CLOUD CAT

Caroline Pitcher likes writing books best of all. She also likes walking her dog, looking at hills and the sea, listening to music, baking cakes and making soup.

One morning, when she was looking at a hillside, she thought of a story for a picture book. It flowed on and on and became the *Cloud Cat* quartet . . .

Cloud Cat won a Writer's Award for work-in-progress from East Midlands Arts.

ALSO BY CAROLINE PITCHER

11 o'Clock Chocolate Cake

Mine

Silkscreen

CAROLINE PITCHER

CLOUD CAT

EGMONT

In memory of Alexander Beardsley (Al)

EGMONT
We bring stories to life

First published in Great Britain 2005
by Egmont Books Limited
239 Kensington High Street,
London W8 6SA

Text copyright © 2005 Caroline Pitcher
Illustration copyright © 2005 David Wyatt

The moral rights of the author and the illustrator have been asserted

ISBN 1 4052 0849 X

3 5 7 9 10 8 6 4 2

A CIP catalogue record for this title is available from the British Library

Typeset by Avon DataSet Ltd, Bidford on Avon, Warwickshire
Printed and bound in Great Britain
by the CPI Group

CONTENTS

CHAPTER 1

DARKNESS SPREADS

Luka watched the young woman's face as she painted the picture. He liked her eyebrows. They were smooth and curved. Her skin looked soft as an apricot.

Her name was Imogen. She came to the orphanage to look after the children. Luka had told her all about his dream. She had listened to him with her head on one side and when he finished, she said, 'That's an amazing dream, Luka. I want to paint a picture of it.' She had fetched her brush and little box and began to paint.

As he watched, a dark spot appeared on her cheek. It grew and grew. The dark spot spread until it covered her face. The darkness spread everywhere. Imogen disappeared.

Now Luka couldn't see her at all. He could hear her voice calling, 'Luka? What's wrong?'

The darkness began to ebb away. Slowly, Imogen's face appeared again as if it was underwater, deep down in a pond. There were no real colours left, just shades of light and dark. The darkness waited. It would not clear away completely.

'Are you all right?' she asked.

'My eyes keep going funny.'

'That's because you're going blind,' announced Aidan-who-had-to-be-carried-everywhere. 'You'll be no help to me if you can't see, Luka. Has the room gone all black?'

'No, Aidan,' said Luka. 'I can see your fat moon face quite clearly.'

This wasn't true. All he could see of Aidan was a pale disc. No eyes or nose or mouth. The room was colour-less. Over in the corner, little phantoms flitted among wobbling towers. Luka knew that the towers were built of wooden bricks. He heard clattering and shrieks of laughter as the children sent their city of bricks spilling across the floor. He listened to the silence as they held their breath and concentrated upon building it up again.

Luka laid his head down on the table. The wood felt rough against his cheek. He closed his eyes and pretended to sleep, but his mind was in turmoil, full of tumbling thoughts. I don't want to spend my life alone in the dark, not yet. I can't stand it.

He wrapped his arms around his head to keep out the thoughts. They buzzed in his mind like wasps around a plum tree that burrow into the soft fruit. He made himself think about his dream instead.

But as he sat there, trying to concentrate, the whispering began. No one else heard it, not Imogen or Eva who worked with the orphans, not Aidan or any of the other children. Only Luka.

It wasn't the first time he'd heard it. The whispering was coming from somewhere above him. It sounded like the hissing noise the water made in the lead pipes at home.

Luka had not dared tell anyone about the whispering, not even his big brother Jez. It was louder this morning. He could hear the words and he wished he couldn't.

'*Idiot. Saphead. Moonraker. My mother knows all about you. She knows who you really are.*'

CHAPTER 2

THE WHISPERER

The Whisperer hung upside down in the orphanage roof. His long feet were hooked over a rafter. He swayed gently. His sleeves hung in tatters from his skinny arms. The Whisperer often hung like this. He could even fall asleep upside down.

Below him there was a spyhole in the ceiling. It had taken him hours to make, gouging away at the rotten yellow plaster with a sharpened stick. He scratched it out soundlessly, his heart beating fast in case he dislodged a blob of plaster that might land on someone's head. Then they would look up and see him!

Through this spyhole, he watched Luka pretending

to be asleep.

'I hate you, little boy!' he whispered. 'I don't know why my mother thinks about you all the time.'

He began to work his cheeks in and out, gathering spit with a soft sucking noise, until he had two big pools of hot spit gathered, one in each cheek.

He was an accomplished spitter. All his life he had watched his mother spitting at anything that moved. She could shower folk with orange spots until they looked like salamanders. Sometimes in the night he dared to aim at the Bone Cracker as it slept, up in their rafters. Usually he missed, much to his relief.

Now the spit flowed to the front of his mouth. He sucked it back again to make sure he had enough and then aimed hard.

It was supposed to land on Luka's cheek. Instead it landed on the back of his hand. The hand twitched but the boy did not even open his eyes.

'You're just pretending to be asleep,' hissed the Whisperer. 'But you won't forget my words. They'll stay in your head, they will. They'll be there forever. Little idiot!'

As if he was on a swing, the Whisperer began to work his body from the waist. He swung higher and higher until he grabbed the rafter and pulled himself up. He wriggled on his stomach across the rafters and out through the gape in the roof. His feet gripped the tiles and he stood up, peering round at the white world, the ruined village, the trees in the forest heavy with snow and the mountains in the distance. He shivered and shook, not from cold, but because the wide world held horrors for him.

'You will never have to see all this!' he cried. '*Idiot!*'

The Whisperer bent his knees and stuck his arms back so that the sleeves hung away from his elbows like ragged feathers. Giving a little yelp, he dropped to the ground and ran away on his long thin feet. Soon the snow fell and covered his footprints.

CHAPTER 3

THE DRAGON AT THE OVEN

'Jez! Let me come to the bakery with you today, please!' pleaded Luka, pulling at his brother's sleeve.

Jez snatched his arm away. 'Get back in your blankets. Your bus won't be here for a couple of hours yet. Can't you see it's still dark?'

'No. I can't.'

'Oh. Sorry,' mumbled Jez. 'But it's so early! Didn't you sleep well?'

'An owl kept me awake. There was an owl hooting right outside my window all night long. I got up and tried to see it but there was just dark.'

Jez laughed. 'An owl? We've lived through years of

war. We've had guns and bombs and screaming, but now an owl keeps you awake? Owls don't shoot rifles; they don't hurl grenades.'

'But they hoot so you have to listen.'

'If you say so, Luka . . . Do you want something to eat now?'

'No. Big Katrin will give me something delicious at the bakery.'

'Crafty! So why don't you want to go to the orphanage today? I thought you liked this new woman who works there. What's her name?'

'Imogen. I do like her. She says funny things, like, "When you are down, the only way is up." She has a lovely face and a long, long plait and her skin is like apricots. You should come and meet her.'

'What colour are her eyes? I like girls with blue eyes,' said Jez, swaggering across the room for his jacket.

'I can't tell what colour they are.'

'Well, I don't have time to go around meeting people,' grumbled Jez. 'Someone has to go out to work and look after you and the dog and –'

'All right, all right, don't go on at me!' cried Luka. 'I

just want to come to the bakery today to see if Syrup's kittens have grown.'

'You can't see –' began Jez. He stopped himself and sighed. 'Oh, I suppose you can come. But you mustn't stop me working. I've just got some kind of order back in my life again. It's called a routine.'

'Is that what you wished for at New Year, Jez? A routine? Is that what you wrote down on your twist of paper and hid?'

'You're not supposed to ask about the New Year wishes,' said Jez. 'I saw you trying to scrawl something on your bit of paper, but I'm not asking *you* to tell me what it was!'

Luka smiled that faraway smile. It annoyed Jez. Luka was keeping something secret from him. 'If you're coming with me, *pest*, you need to wash your face. It's got yesterday's dinner all over it.'

'Of course I will, Jez,' said Luka meekly. He wanted to wash his hands too, especially as he was going to the bakery. The kitchen where they lived was covered in grease as thick as treacle and a maze of green mould grew up the wall by the stairs. He felt his way across to the sink and dipped his fingers into the bowl of water. The cold made him gasp. He thought, maybe my eyes will work properly at the bakery. Maybe my sight only goes when I'm at the orphanage and I hear the whispering? Well, it's all going to be different. Tomorrow I am going to change everything!

When Luka thought about what he was going to do, he began to tremble, because it was so exciting. It was frightening, too.

It was still dark when they left for the bakery. Jez shut the door on the whining dog. Off they went, along the snowy street, with Luka clinging to Jez's arm and his feet scuffing the ground. There was not much of the street left. Over the years, war had wiped most of the village away and left ruins, like the children's toppled towers of bricks at the orphanage. Jez and Luka never really understood who was fighting, or why. Now their land was thick with soldiers from other countries and it had changed names so many times no one could remember what it was called in the first place.

A big hare crossed their path, causing Luka to stumble so that he fell to his knees in the snow. The hare ran to the side of the street and sat up, looking at them.

'Geddout, hare!' shouted Jez. 'You're lucky I haven't got a gun with me!'

The hare twitched its ears and loped away behind a tumble of stones.

'Are you all right?' said Jez, brushing the snow off Luka's knees. 'Maybe that's what the dog was sniffing after this morning. She went mad when I let her out into the yard.'

'Are you sure it was just a hare? Or an owl?' said Luka. 'Come on, Jez! I'm so cold and I'm hungry. I want to get to the bakery.' I want to see if my eyes work there.

At the end of the broken street was the bakery. It was a tall house with a cat-slide roof and a blue door, and it leaned out from a corner, as if it wondered whether to fall down like its ruined friends. Luka loved the bakery. He helped Jez heave open the door and breathed in the warm smell. So many buns and apples stuffed with honey and raisins had been baked there for so many years that even the stones in the wall were steeped in the warm, spicy cinnamon sweetness and the tiles in the roof were full of it.

Just inside the doorway, Luka stopped and grabbed Jez's hand. He saw a fat white dragon, breathing fire. After the grey snow light in the street, the bakery was pitch black, all except for this shape crouched in the middle of the room. By its head was a furnace of flickering red and yellow flames. Luka felt the heat pounding his legs.

'Luka! I didn't know you were coming today!' The dragon stood up from the oven and hurried across the room. It was Dimitri, his white apron tied tightly across his stomach and his tall baker's hat pulled down so that it almost touched his thick black eyebrows. He picked Luka up and swung him round.

'You're light as a feather, Luka! Doesn't your brother feed you?'

'Of course I do,' said Jez in a hurt voice, 'but he just pushes the food round his plate until it's cold and then he gives it to the dog.'

Dimitri pulled out a chair and sat Luka on it by the big trestle table.

'Wait till the first batch of bread is out, Luka. Can you smell it baking? Then we'll feed you up. You'll be a fine figure of a man. Like me!' He smacked his stomach. It sounded like someone bursting a paper bag.

Luka listened to the fire crackle, and the shutting of the little iron door on the firebox. He heard Jez wash his hands then set about kneading and punching the dough. Luka loved that sound. The big doors of the bread oven were opened; the heat rushed out. He heard Dimitri slide in another tray of bread and shut the door again. Then Dimitri poured milk into a cup. Luka heard him dip in the brush and then stroke the top of the batch of milk loaves. He heard Jez chopping, the rasp of the grater and the knife slicing. Jez would be making little mountains of toppings to sprinkle on Dimitri's Just For Us loaves. They would eat one later, warm and crusty with melted cheese. Luka breathed in the scent of the herbs and blinked at the onion. It made his eyes water but it did not clear the darkness.

The bakery door burst open. Big Katrin's boots stamped on the mat, one! two! Then Luka felt himself wrapped in her arms as if he were her cub. He pressed his face against her tickly fur coat. He liked the smell. It was cinnamon mixed with warm, powdery Big Katrin.

'But what about Syrup?' he asked her.

'She's asleep on Katrin's clean washing in the basket by the back fire!' called Dimitri.

Big Katrin tut-tutted. Luka heard her boots squeal as she strode across the flagstones. A moment later Luka felt the warm weight of the cat on his knee. One after the other, he felt the lightness of the six kittens. Their tiny paws kneaded his leg. Syrup's deep purr vibrated through her soft sides like a dynamo, and Luka's fingertips traced the trembling purrs of her kittens – when they could stay still long enough.

'Hey, get your claws out of my legs, you lot!' he giggled.

Dimitri lifted Syrup gently down and shooed the kittens, who plopped down on to the floor and darted away after their mother.

Dimitri placed a mound of dough on the table in front of Luka. He paused, then took Luka's hands and placed them on it.

'Here you are,' he said. 'You can get to work on that!'

Luka loved the feel of the dough. It was soft and stretchy, like elastic, and it grew warm as he worked it.

'I'm making moons and stars and fish,' he said.

'Good,' replied Dimitri. 'And can you do a bird just for me? I'm missing the swallows. Curvy wings and nice tail streamers please . . .' Dimitri crossed to the oven and opened the door.

'Hurry up with the Just For Us, Jez,' he called.

'I've nearly finished,' said Jez, sprinkling the chopped herbs on the loaves. He loved making Just For Us loaves. It was a rhythm, a routine, a pattern, and he just couldn't go wrong. First he laid the thin onion rings on the top of the loaf. Next he dredged a layer of grated cheese and finished with a fine green sprinkling of rosemary and thyme.

His eyes were watering from the strong juices that seeped from the cut onions. He blinked hard. There were distinct rumbling sounds from his stomach. He had had nothing to eat today and the prospect of the hot, aromatic bread was almost too much to bear. You could work in worse places in wartime than a bakery, thought Jez.

'Excuse my tummy rumbling, Dimitri!' he called. He turned to wipe his streaming eyes on a towel, looked up and at once screamed, 'Luka! No! You'll burn to death!'

He flung himself across the room, feeling as if it took forever, until his hands grabbed Luka and dragged him away from the oven. Bread rolls flew out of Luka's arms and rolled across the flagstones.

'What do you think you're doing, Luka?' shouted Jez, slamming him down on the chair. 'Your whole side was just about to touch the oven! You'd lose your skin. *Idiot*!'

Luka's face grew red. *Idiot*. His eyes filled with tears but he blinked them away. He said, 'Dimitri wanted a bread bird – a swallow. I was going to put my rolls in to bake for breakfast.'

'No you weren't! You were going to set yourself on fire! Luka, will you face the fact that you can't see?'

There was a long silence. Dimitri picked up the rolls, blew across their tops and set them carefully on the oven shelf. Big Katrin glanced around her and found some silver ribbon that was supposed to tie up cake boxes. She gave this to Luka and placed a couple of kittens on his knee again. Without a word, she clonked upstairs to make more tea.

Luka sat in silence while the kittens batted the dangling ribbon with their small cushioned paws. Dimitri grabbed Luka and lifted him up on his shoulders.

'Jez did not mean to shout at you, Luka. You're all he's got. He couldn't bear it if anything happened to you. Isn't that right, Jez?'

'Something *is* going to happen to me,' stated Luka. 'Soon.'

'Don't say things like that!' snapped Jez.

Dimitri took Luka down off his shoulders and sat him on the table before him.

'Nothing is going to happen to you, Luka. Now give me a hug.'

Luka leaned forward and reached up to Dimitri. They had a good tight cuddle and then –

'Dimitri! Look what you've done!' laughed Jez.

'Oh no! I've sat you down on Katrin's pie. Quick! Before she comes back!'

They giggled as Dimitri tried to mend the pie, panicking, pressing the pastry together again over the apples so that Big Katrin shouldn't see what had happened. She did, of course. She came back with the tea tray just as Dimitri was trying to flute the pastry edge with his thumb the way he'd seen her do it, but making a terrible mess.

Katrin took up her rolling pin and chased the baker round the table until he fell to his knees and begged for mercy.

'You look as if you're asking Katrin to marry you, Dimitri!' called Jez.

'Never!' roared the baker. 'Young, handsome and single! That's me!'

'You're single, all right!' said Jez. 'Come here, Luka. Your bottom is covered in sugar.'

Big Katrin chuckled. Her smile faded as she remembered who had stopped her on the way to work that morning. Three strangers. Two men, one woman, her face shadowed by a hood trimmed with white ermine fur. The woman bent close and asked, 'Where do the children live? We have been told to collect up the orphans.'

The hairs on the back of Katrin's neck rose.

'We will pay well,' the woman said. 'Where are they?'

Buying children? Katrin stepped out into the street, raised her arm and pointed down the road out of the village.

'You mean they have already been taken?' cried the woman.

Katrin nodded fiercely.

The three hesitated, shooting glances between themselves. At last they turned, and set off down the road. Only when they were out of sight did Katrin hurry on her way to the bakery, thinking, how long before they come back from their wild goose chase?

On the way home, Luka asked Jez, 'Is Dimitri really young and handsome?'

Jez laughed. 'He's bald. He has two eyebrows that look as if someone has stuck two black hairy caterpillars over his eyes. He's not quite as young as he'd like to think, Luka.'

'Is he the same age as Dad? They are friends, aren't they?'

'I think so' muttered Jez. 'Think they were, anyway.'

'Then why isn't Dimitri married? Why doesn't he marry Katrin?'

'I don't know, Luka! He talks enough for both of them, but they'd be an odd couple. She's as big as a bear, and he's so small and round. Walk faster. I want to get indoors and –'

'Wait!' shouted Luka. Jez blinked and saw that

they had reached the chestnut tree.

'What is it *now*?' he groaned.

'There's a notice on the tree. It says,

LOST – A VERY BIG CAT'

'Luka, listen to me. There's nothing there,' said Jez.

'Yes, there is! The letters are in green ink. They're decorated with leaves and buds. The writing twists like honeysuckle, all round the word "CAT". Look!'

'How can you read a notice when you can't even see it? You can't see this world properly, so you're inventing your own. Come on, you should have an early night, after sleeping so badly last night.'

To Jez's surprise, Luka nodded. 'I think I'll go straight to bed after supper,' he said. 'Then I will be fresh and bright for tomorrow.'

'Tomorrow? Have you got a busy day at the orphanage, then?' teased Jez.

Luka turned his face away and smiled to himself.

CHAPTER 4

INTO THE BLANKET CHEST

Luka was awake all night long, by the fire where he and Jez slept. The owl was hooting in the bare fruit trees again, but that was not why. He kept himself awake on purpose. He breathed deeply and loudly and squeezed his eyes tight shut so that Jez would think he was fast asleep.

At last he heard what he was waiting for. It came padding out of the trees, through the hole in the wall and into the yard. It snuffled at the door of his house. Luka heard it, *chuff. . . chuff*. It was waiting on the other side of the door, waiting for *him*!

Early next morning, Luka listened to his brother

getting up and leaving for the bakery. After Jez was gone, he waited, huddled in his nest of blankets, for as long as he could bear. Then he got dressed and felt his way up the staircase. He had to be careful. Jez had removed some of the stairs to burn, and the floorboards were rotten, with dynasties of mice living underneath. Luka crawled over them – on his tummy because of the gaps – until he reached the blanket chest.

Jez told him that their great-grandfather had made it from an oak tree, carving acorns with little impy faces and leaves all around the lid. Luka liked to trace the faces with his fingers and feel their pointed noses and grins.

It was the only piece of wood Jez had not chopped up to burn on the fire this cruel winter.

Now it made the perfect place to hide. Luka lifted the lid and climbed inside. There was only just enough room because the chest was full of scratchy blankets they had been given in the war. Luka let the lid fall shut with a big BANG! He was so excited, his tummy felt as if it was full of soft butterflies. He listened, hard. First he heard the dog sniff at the lid. Then he began to hear those taunts. The whispering. *Idiot! My mother knows who you really are . . .*

So he made himself think about his dream instead, until the words were pushed to one side.

And there was the bus! He heard it changing gear on the hill, coming to take him to the orphanage for yet another long day. The engine coughed and spluttered and died away. Luka heard Peter, the driver, cough too. Peter coughed and spat all the time because he smoked too many cigarettes. Luka hated that smell on the bus in the mornings.

There was a knock on the door – a *come on, hurry up!* knock. The dog barked. Luka held his breath. Another knock. Another bark. At last the engine started again, and the bus chugged away. Luka let his breath go. Phew! With his lips against the scratchy blankets, he said, 'I'm very sorry, Imogen, but I can't come to the orphanage today. There's something else I have to do. I am going to make everything change. You'll see!'

When Luka could no longer hear the bus, he climbed out of the blanket chest. He went downstairs. He felt all around his nest of blankets for his boots. He pulled them on. They were still soaking from yesterday's snow and they clung to his ankles like wet hands. Luka wished that he had left them in front of the fire last night to dry.

He knew that the dog was wagging her tail, because a draught of cold air rushed past his face. She thought they were both going out somewhere.

'No, get out of the way or I'll fall over you, dog!' Luka told her. He dragged the chair over to the back door and stumbled up on to it. He felt for the bolts. The top bolt was stiff. The bottom one was easy, but he had to tug hard at the door because the wood had warped with damp.

Jez would be almost at the bakery by now. They were kind to him there, but Luka knew he was different from them. He was different from everyone. He could not go on living like everyone else did. He had to try another kind of life. He knew that now.

Luka gave one last great tug, and the door sprang open. *Ouch!* The white world rushed straight in at him, dazzling his eyes as if the snow was made of sequins.

'STOP IT!' cried Luka. It was blinding him

completely. He screwed up his eyes and concentrated.

There was a trail of dark roses in the snow.

Luka stuck out his right arm, with his hand held straight. He turned his hand over and moved to place his palm in the dark rose. It was the wrong way up. He got up off the step, went down into the yard and turned back towards the doorstep. With his fingertips, he traced the indent of a round pad. He touched it with his palm. He traced four strong toes, but found no place for his thumb.

'I wish you could see this, Jez,' he whispered. 'Paws three times as big as my hands!'

He stood up and went inside to fetch his gloves, his lunch that Jez had packed for him to take to the orphanage, and the honey-coloured drum. He stuffed them down into his backpack and pulled it over his shoulders. The dog scrambled out from under the table and tried to come with him. Luka heaved the door shut against her, then squinted hard at the ground and followed the trail of paw prints all the way round the yard and back again, and out through the hole in the wall.

In the kitchen the dog whined and scratched at the door. There was the sharp smell of some beast outside. *Danger.* During the night she had heard sounds from way back in her dog memory. *Howling.* But it was not the howling of dogs. The hair round her neck rose into a stiff ruff from fear.

CHAPTER 5

THE CINNAMON HOUSE

Jez hurried along to work, glancing to either side of
him, listening hard.

You never knew if there was a sniper behind a door,
or in the shell of a house, until you heard the whine of
his rifle, or the cry of his victim. There was always an
enemy. You were never sure who it was. This enemy lit
matches in people's gas canisters so that they roared into
flames. This enemy hid up in the church tower and fired
when the bells tolled, stole chickens and sheep, ripped
cabbages out of the fields, dug up potatoes, plunged the
village into darkness and put poison in the wells and the
water pipes. This enemy caused the screaming that woke

Jez and Luka early, making them bury their heads under their pillows because they could not bear the sound.

Yet, after all this, the chestnut tree was still there. Jez stopped underneath it, and gazed up into the web of branches. He could see buds shiny as little hooves. If only they would swell and open! He remembered how in spring the hands of green leaves held white blossom candles, and how in autumn his father lifted him high up to reach the green chestnuts. Split open the spiny case and there was the glossy nut hiding in velvet. Soak it in vinegar, load it on string and let battle begin! Jez had been school champion three years running.

Now the chestnut tree was just a dark skeleton fringed with frozen white.

Jez sighed, shook his father's smiling face right out of his head, and hurried on to the tall house that smelled of spices.

'Late again, Jez! I'll have to dock your wages!'

'Sorry,' said Jez, hanging his jacket to thaw out on a chair near the oven.

'I'm only joking!' said Dimitri. 'I was worried when you didn't turn up.'

'Nothing happened!' said Jez. He washed his hands in the cold water from the tap. Dimitri had already plaited dough into long loaves and laid them on trays. Jez brushed them with milk and sprinkled them with poppy seeds.

The street door swung open and a blast of icy air roared into the bakery. Big Katrin stamped her red boots, one! two! and slammed the door shut. She pulled off her blue scarf and shook out her hair. Snow flew on to the stone floor and winked as it melted. She reached inside her coat and slapped a folded newspaper down on the table. She looked at Dimitri and she looked at Jez. Then she stomped off upstairs.

'Fix us some tea, Katrin!' the baker shouted. 'Tea upstairs, coffee downstairs! That's the way it's always been and that's the way it is!'

That's the way it is, mouthed Jez to himself. They said the same things every day. Jez liked that. He slid the tray of poppy-seed bread into the oven and closed the door. He set to work on the next batch, up and down the rows of plaited loaves waiting for him. This time, he brushed the tops with olive oil and sprinkled them with snips of rosemary and thyme.

CLOP-CLOP! CLOP-CLOP!

'Is it a pony and trap? Is it a bear in clogs?' cried Dimitri. 'No, it's Katrin!'

Down the stairs she came, bearing the brown teapot on a tray like a crown on a cushion for a king. The three of them sat at the table, their hands wrapped round the warm mugs. The tea soothed Jez's stomach.

'How is your little brother today?' asked Dimitri.

Jez sighed. 'He's so reckless sometimes, Dimitri. He scares me. He rushes at things, as if he has nothing to lose. His eyesight is far, far worse, but he will never admit it.'

'It must have been the shock of losing your mother and father,' said Dimitri. 'You know Katrin and I will do whatever we can for you both.'

Jez said quickly, 'Thanks. Dimitri, I know why Luka cannot see. I know how it happened. Luka *mustn't* know. And I don't want to talk about my mother and father.'

Big Katrin listened and pictured Luka, so small and cheeky, with no mother to hold him in her arms, no father to carry him through the village high on his shoulders. Sometimes Katrin tried to clean up their house for them, but it was full of sadness, a house mourning its people, and it was too far gone for her to clean, with its walls like maps of damp, and its rotten floorboards. Katrin sighed, and picked up the news-paper. She unfolded it and smoothed it out on the table. She looked at Dimitri, and then at Jez. On the front page of the paper was a photograph.

'It's just a snowdrift,' said Jez. 'So what's special about that?'

Dimitri popped his spectacles on the end of his nose and looked again.

'It's not just a snowdrift, Jez. It's this wild beast on the loose. Haven't you heard about it? It took a sheep and dragged it up into a tree. It ate some and then left the other half there for later.'

'Rubbish!' cried Jez. 'It'll be a hungry fox or a wild dog, or someone nicking food to feed their hungry children. They just want to put something different from war in the newspaper, that's all. And this paper is four days old!'

Dimitri stabbed his floury finger at a faint shadow in a corner of the photograph.

'That's a beast,' he said.

'That's a snowdrift, Dimitri!' guffawed Jez.

'Maybe it is. Maybe it isn't. But you'd better be careful, living out on the edge of the village. Watch out for your little brother.'

'Luka will be safely at the orphanage by now!' protested Jez. 'This new Imogen will be fussing round him.'

'Good. The more people that look out for him the better. There is badness on the move,' warned Dimitri. 'Katrin saw that Vaskalia woman yesterday. She was here, peeping in to the bakery. Katrin thinks she was looking for Luka.'

'Why? I'll never let her near him!' cried Jez. 'I haven't seen her for years. Not since that time at school.'

'What time at school?'

Jez mumbled, 'It was horrible.'

'Tell me!'

'Dimitri, it was years ago. It happened before the fighting began. When the school was still open. Her son, Simlin, made my life hell. He was as spiteful as a stinging nettle. He – he used to lead the other children after me, and get them to pull faces and call me names.

He told them not to play football with me if I asked. In class he stuck pins in my back. Then one day – it was just after Dad h-had gone – he began to whisper behind his hand, just loud enough for everyone to hear. He was whispering about Luka. Said he was a muggins, a moron, a wall-eyed idiot!'

'What a snake! Luka was so little then. What happened?'

'I slapped him hard. It made a red mark like a poppy on his milksop cheek! I felt much better. He wasn't going to call *my* little brother names ever again!'

'I don't blame you, Jez,' said Dimitri, 'but I know that's not the end of the story, not if Vaskalia was involved.'

Jez sighed. 'You're right. Next morning, the other kids cried, "It's Simlin's mother, the doll woman! She's come to school. She has the evil eye!" and they scattered right away from her. Up she came, dumpy as a wooden doll. I tried to hurry past, but she shot out her arm and grabbed me so I could smell her eggy breath – FWARF! And she cursed me, Dimitri. I'd never heard such language! Some words I did not even know existed, but I knew they were filthy. She threatened me with werewolves and walking corpses if I did not say sorry to her son. Then she spat upon my foot. It was lime green, Dimitri!'

Dimitri glanced at Big Katrin. Her eyes were full of worry.

He said, 'What did your teacher do?'

'Nothing. All of a sudden the teacher was nowhere to be seen. I slunk across the playground to Simlin. He was smirking. I said, "Sorry." For three days, my wrist had blood round it like a bracelet and I had a blister like an orange mushroom on my toe.'

Dimitri said, 'I wish you'd told me this before, Jez. I did not know you had already made an enemy of Vaskalia. Nobody should get on the wrong side of her, least of all you and Luka, Jez, because bad things happened in the past.'

'What things?'

'Vaskalia wanted to marry your father.'

Jez saw Big Katrin nod. He felt a little twinge of fear, because her face looked so serious, her eyes so dark and grave.

Dimitri went on, 'Vaskalia knows something about

your family. She wanted your father for herself. But your father went travelling and he returned with your lovely mother. Vaskalia hated that. She's jealousy incarnate, Jez. She hardly ever goes out of her funny little house. So if she *is* up in the village . . . be careful, very careful!'

Jez cried, 'Dimitri, *please*! You're scaring me. I'll keep Luka safe. I'll keep him away from Vaskalia, and safe from this wild beast.'

CHAPTER 6

THE BOOK OF DANCES

'Why am I still crawling on all fours?'

Luka stood up in the snow, blinking at the paw prints. The creature must be as big as the lion in the book his mother had read to him every night, years ago, before the dull boom of war, the dust-burst explosions and the crack of rifle fire began. It was a special book, with a cover the blue of gentian flowers, about unicorns, griffins and dragons. The creatures danced. They were like animals, and like people too. When the book was closed, the edges of the pages shone together as steadfast gold as her wedding ring.

People fell out of Luka's world. He did not know

what had happened to his father. Jez would not talk about it. Soon after his father disappeared, Luka grew ill. His sight began to fade. Worst of all, his mother pined. And then she was taken away from them.

In his mind's eye Luka often saw a picture of himself, standing behind glass, resting his palms against it. On the other side of the glass, Jez and Dimitri and Big Katrin, Imogen and the children from the orphanage played and read and baked and drew. They looked into each other's eyes and mirrored each other's frowns and smiles.

He could never join them, or share what they did. He lived outside their world.

But he knew he could enter a much bigger world of brilliant colours, a world with different creatures. They travelled with a man who had hair as bright as frost. Luka's favourite of these creatures was the great cloud cat. Its fine thick fur was like a white sky marked with dark-edged clouds and it could leap across chasms and roam wherever it wanted. Luka longed to be like that and last night the cloud cat had come looking for him, padding round his house in the dismal village, leaving its tracks to show him the way out.

'Today it's all going to change!' cried Luka as he followed the trail of paw prints through the snow, arms out from his sides to help his balance.

'I'm like a penguin,' he giggled.

Far beyond the village there were mountains. To get to them he would have to go up the hills first. Jez often warned Luka against going that way. 'If you take the wrong turning from the hills you come to a rope bridge, over the Depths of Lumb, the giant cracks in the earth that plunge deep, deep down. If you fall in, you'll never come out the same.'

I'm sure the paw prints won't go down to the Depths of Lumb! Luka thought. He let them lead him on up the hillside.

At first he enjoyed the rhythm of his slow, heavy steps in the snow. The snow hushed everything, but Luka's eyes were beginning to feel sore from the wind and snow. He wanted to shut his eyelids.

'Jez, I wish you were here to tell me what everything looks like,' he said, wanting to hear a voice even if it was his own. Why can I only see the cloud cat's paw prints?

Where are the man's footprints, and why haven't the other creatures left their tracks?'

Luka struggled on, although his lungs were beginning to burn with each breath. His chest heaved. His throat felt raw. The hush was closing in on him. It was hard to breathe.

He stopped. He could no longer see the cloud cat's paw prints.

There was something standing at his side. He knew it was taller than he was. It did not move.

'Are you frozen too?' Luka asked. It did not answer.

He held out his hand, slowly. It was a tree. No. It felt too smooth for a tree.

It was a post, covered in ice. There was a rope leading away from it. Luka put out his other hand. There was a post on that side too, and a rope. Luka peeled off first one glove, then the other, and laid them down in the snow by the posts. Then he knelt down.

'Logs. They're little logs with gaps in between.'

He stuck his fingers into a gap in the wood. He could waggle them at the other side. There was twisted rope binding the logs together. He gave the logs a little push. They swayed.

With a sinking heart, Luka realised where he was.

The rope bridge.

He could hear Jez's warning voice in his head, telling him, *Don't go over the rope bridge, Luka. If you fall into the Depths of Lumb, you'll never come out the same.*

Luka blinked hard, peering towards the bridge through the fuzzy snow. There! Halfway across, the snow was all scuffed up.

'The Cloud Cat came this way!'

Luka had to follow. It would be all right. But as soon as he set foot on the bridge, it began to shake. He grasped the rope with both hands to steady himself.

The bridge creaked and groaned and swayed. Luka gripped the rope tighter. In his mind he saw Imogen's strong plait of hair and wished he was holding on to that instead, because his hands told him that *this* rope was thin and frayed. The wind was blasting down the gorge. Luka stopped. No, keep going, keep going and get to the other side before the rope breaks.

At last his foot felt ground again, a narrow path

leading downwards. A vicious wind skimmed the snow and blasted it along, hiding any tracks there may have been.

There was a rustling sound down on the snow near him. What on earth could it be? Luka was almost too tired to care. All he wanted to do was lie down and go to sleep. Maybe just for a moment? No! He knew that would mean death. If you went to sleep in this snow you would freeze to death. He passed his hand over his eyes. Hard little icicles hung from his hair. Ice crusted his nostrils. Tears froze on his cheeks.

'Everything will be fine once I find the Cloud Cat!'

The path began to go up, steeply. He felt bumps under the snow, steps or big stones. He couldn't be sure. Somehow he was on all fours again, crawling up, his hands and feet scrabbling for safe holds, his stomach shocked with cold, his eyes screwed shut against snow and tears.

Suddenly there were no more stones. Luka hesitated. He tried to get his balance. He stood up, wobbling. He opened his eyes but found that he was looking through two kaleidoscopes. Each eye was a circle of white splintered into prisms. Worse, he was hit from all sides by spiteful little winds, whining and stabbing at his face. In the winds, Luka heard it again. The whispering. *Idiot. Idiot!* He crouched down again as if he was praying, while the winds picked on him like a gang of bullies in a playground.

He heard a sob, hanging in the air. It was *his*. It sobbed, 'Jez? JEZ!'

The winds changed direction. Luka knew at once that it wasn't only wind rushing at him, brushing his forehead and buffeting his cheek, but some thing that was alive. *Wingbeats.* The thing was big. It could fly. And it didn't like him. Whatever it was waited patiently for just the right moment. It waited for him to be at his weakest. Then it would attack him. The power of the wingbeats horrified him.

'Don't, please!' he begged, battering the air to be rid of it. Useless. The thing was immediately out of his reach. He wrapped his arms around his head as it flew full at him.

Luka heard a cry, and knew that he was falling down to the darkest place.

CHAPTER 7

EMPTINESS

In the darkening afternoon, Jez trudged home. He clutched a bag of warm scones and a pat of butter wrapped carefully in muslin by Big Katrin. He licked his lips as he thought of them. Luka would ask for jam. Raspberry jam had always been his favourite, but no one could think of growing raspberries in wartime. Big Katrin made sweet plum jam which Luka loved. He scooped out big dollops of it on to his bread. Jez hoped there was still some left in the jar for the scones tonight.

The snow bowled through the ruined streets, covering the rubble and turning it into castles from a fairy tale. The winter had come months before and never left. The world was wrong. It had gone tilting away from light and warmth and it had forgotten to tilt back again.

Jez heard creaking. He glanced fearfully over his shoulder, but decided it was just a roof complaining under the heavy snow. There had been no fighting for some weeks now.

'There's no wild beast in the village,' he told himself, 'and it is still so cold that Vaskalia and her son will be huddled indoors over their fire.'

He hurried on, then caught his breath harshly in his throat and stopped short.

A bulky shape came swaying out of an alleyway. It lumbered down the street towards Jez. It was joined to the figure of a man by a tight rein. He was stumbling after the animal as it picked its way fearfully over the treacherous snowy cobblestones. Jez hesitated. Should he turn and run?

He saw that the man was nervous too, cowering against his beast of burden as if he wished he could disappear. Jez now saw that the bulky beast was a donkey, laden down with paniers. Sitting on its back was a young woman, wrapped up against the cold.

The man's head was bound with scarves but Jez saw his frightened eyes. They were the shape of almonds. Jez knew then that the man was one of the mountain people. They had suffered more than most in the fighting, but Jez wondered why the man and the woman were trying to escape now.

Something about them spoke to Jez, and said, *Please don't let them come to any harm.* He turned to watch them swaying down the road. In spite of his wariness he called after them, 'I wish you a safe journey!' The man did not turn, but raised his hand in acknowledgement.

Jez thought of fire and warm scones with melting butter and hurried on to his own house.

He unlocked the front door and burst in. 'Luka? I'm back! With scones and BUT-TER!'

The dog slunk across the floor and lay at his feet. Her ears were set back, pulling the skin away from her eyes.

'What's the matter with you? Your eyes are bulging out like humbugs. LUKA? *LUKA!*'

Jez's voice hung in the empty rooms.

He ran upstairs. He looked around. He wrenched up the lid of the blanket chest, where he often found Luka curled up, hiding. But Luka wasn't there today. *Perhaps the bus has got stuck in the snow. Or perhaps he's still at the home, chatting to that Imogen. Little devil! The scones will get quite cold.*

Jez kicked the chest. He stomped downstairs. Someone had pulled back the bolts on the door into the yard. Jez wrenched it open and blinked out. Fresh snow covered the ground. He pulled the door shut, bolting it now, turned, treading on the dog's paw so that she yelped. Jez grumbled at her and stumbled his way out into the streets again, down the hill and across the ruined village to the orphanage. The dog ran behind him with her belly low to the ground.

The orphans lived in the old school, a crumbling building with dips in the roof and boarded-up windows. When the fighting started, people would not let their children out of their sight. The school closed down. Jez could remember before that. He remembered sitting at a wooden desk with names and love hearts carved on the lid, and the teacher shouting at him for not learning his numbers and times-tables and for tangling knots in the thread she gave him to stitch on his square of binca.

Now the front door of the old school was as full of holes as a colander. Men with guns had wanted someone who was hiding inside. They had peppered the door with bullet holes and shattered the small windowpanes faster than boys throwing stones.

Jez hurried inside, scanning the big room for Luka. A little girl with curly black hair knelt on the floor, humming to herself as she built a castle with wooden bricks. She set a row of arches carefully along the top. Another girl sat still, watching her.

Jez saw the row of heavy iron cots in the corner. A child in heavy nappies stood up in one of them, holding the bars as if he was in a cage. He looked through the bars at Jez with huge eyes, but he made no sound.

Jez cleared his throat and called, 'Luka? Where are you? Come on out. It's time to go home.'

The door at the opposite end of the room opened and in walked Imogen, carrying a red-haired boy. Her eyes were dark and full, and immediately made Jez feel clumsy. The red-haired boy leaned forward and poked Jez in the ribs.

'You're looking for Luka, aren't you?' he squealed. 'Well, he didn't come today.'

This must be Aidan-who-has-to-be-carried-every-where. He has no legs. Must have been the war. Luka was right; Aidan's voice is fat.

Aidan narrowed his eyes as if he was sharing a big secret. 'Luka is a bad boy, because he can't see. He thinks we can't see him. He plays that little drum and dances and pretends he's not here. He's very naughty.'

'He's no naughtier than you are, Aidan,' said Imogen. Her voice was low. She had curvy smooth eyebrows that made Jez think of the glossy wings of a swallow. She set Aidan down on a chair. He scowled up at her and stuck out his lower lip. Jez looked at the heavy plait of hair hanging down Imogen's back and remembered the bell rope in the old church.

Imogen said, 'Maybe Luka has gone to meet you from work?'

'Not without the dog,' growled Jez.

'He wants his independence before his sight goes completely.'

'Yeah. That doctor who came with the peacekeepers said it might be – di-jenny-er . . .'

'Degenerative,' she said.

'I know what it's called!' snapped Jez. 'But Luka's luckier than *this* lot of orphans in here. He's got me, he's got the dog and a house and food, and . . .'

'And soon he'll be quite blind. So he's testing the limits.'

'He's testing *my* limits,' grumbled Jez, but he thought, Maybe she's right. He's gone to the bakery on his own to meet me. Jez made up a picture in his mind and concentrated on it; Luka sat at the table in the bakery scoffing buns. Dimitri snored on the settle and Big Katrin beat sugar and butter to ice her cakes. This is what I want every day now. Comfort. Safety. Routine.

Jez sighed. He felt as if he was wearing a heavy belt. From the belt hung little metal effigies of everything he had lost: the bicycle he had been promised, a fishing rod, a football to kick around with his father, the cake for his fourteenth birthday which was the first birthday without his parents, the notes of a song his mother sang in the kitchen as she scored diamond patterns on big potatoes and put them round the sizzling meat, and two tiny metal people – his mother and father. The things he had lost hung like trophies of cold metal, weighing him down and stopping him breathing deeply enough.

He had never thought he might add Luka to his belt.

CHAPTER 8

THE MAN WITH THE
HAIR OF FROST

Imogen said, 'I'll make you some tea and something to eat.'

Jez sat down awkwardly on a child's chair. His bony knees almost touched his chin. The children watched him. They had old, wary faces.

Imogen brought him a bowl full of hot porridge, with a pool of milk and a dollop of damson jam, and a glass of apple tea sweetened with honey. Jez thought, Yes, Luka. Her skin *is* like rosy apricots.

Eva, who worked with Imogen every day, brought the children milk and a box of biscuits. Jez remembered her helping the sour-faced teacher years before. She was always smiling and laughing. She played wonderful games with them, Pirates and Dragon Lair and There Was a Princess Long Ago. Their favourite was What's the Time, Mr Wolf? because Eva could howl and growl like a wolf as she chased them across the playground. Sometimes she just laughed too much to wolf-howl. Early one morning, while Eva was cleaning the classroom ready for them, her house was blown up. Her son was killed as he slept in his bed. The joy fled from Eva's face and she seemed to grow into an old woman. She was stooped and lame. She could not chase anyone. At night she slept on a rug on the floor between the cots.

Now Eva smiled wearily at Jez. He saw that her eyes looked almost washed away by crying.

Aidan lunged for Jez's bowl, chattering angrily like a squirrel. Imogen laughed and fetched him porridge too. Aidan put the bowl right up to his face and his tongue into the bowl and lapped noisily. Imogen turned to Jez and smiled and he felt himself blush. He suddenly wondered what he looked like and tried to smooth down his hair. It felt coarse, even a bit sticky.

He mumbled, 'Sorry. I get upset and cross quickly,

especially with Luka. And don't just tell me to hold my breath and count to ten!'

'Ten is too many, Jez. I get the children to count to seven. They have to think of seven special things. Sometimes it's seven favourite stories. But I never ask them their seven favourite people because their favourite people are often missing. The one they like the best is counting seven good things to eat. They can all do that!'

She giggled softly, and Jez worried that she thought he was a clumsy peasant with no manners who ate his food much too fast.

'You're not from round here, are you? Your voice is different.'

Her smile faded. 'I'm from the south. I couldn't stay in my own town. One day all my family were taken, all my brothers and sisters. I was at college. I found my home was just a heap of stones. So I work here, with these children. I make them a home instead.'

'They must drive you mad!' said Jez, glancing round at the blobs of porridge on Aidan's nose, the hare-eyed boy shaking the bars of his cot, and the little girls squabbling over the bricks.

'They get me through the day. I'm too busy to think much because I have to look after them,' she said. She spoke calmly. She thought about things before she said them. Not like me.

He said, 'I – my parents have gone too.'

'There is always someone to help, Jez. You are not on your own.'

Jez felt tears welling in his eyes. Quick, don't let her see! He swallowed hard and said, 'What did Aidan mean about Luka playing a drum?'

Imogen went over to a cupboard and fetched a small drum. She placed it on the table. It was made of pale wood. Thin hide, the colour of honey, was stretched tight across the wooden circlet. There were bears and wolves and deer with antlers carved in the wood so that they ran round the drum. Stick figures danced and waved their arms, and Jez saw the wigwam shape of a little fire with billows of smoke.

'It's one of a pair of drums but the other one is missing. Luka drums with his palms and fingers. It's like his pulse, or his heart beating. He closes his eyes and concentrates. Sometimes he dances. He wears that fur coat from the dressing-up box. We have to guess which animal he is. He can really lose himself in things, can't he?'

'Yeah, well he's really lost himself this time!' sighed Jez, picking up the drum and turning it round in his hands. He thought of Luka's small, intent face, the skin so thin you could almost see through it. Round his eyes it was like pale crocus petals, veined with mauve.

Imogen said, 'Does he ever tell you about his dreams?'

Luka had tried to tell him, but Jez had ignored him. *I haven't got time for your stories. I've got work and food to worry about!*

'He thinks so much of you, Jez.'

He glanced up. She had a pretty mouth; full, with pointed bows to the lips, like the mouth of the stone angel that used to perch on a high ledge in the village church. His face burned red with embarrassment.

'Here's a watercolour I did of Luka's dream,' said Imogen.

Jez grabbed the picture of a group of figures around a fire.

'That's really good! I've never seen a man with skin

that golden-green colour before. It's like an acorn before it's ripe.'

'Luka said that the man's skin was as golden-green as a russet apple.'

Jez tried to speak but his voice was hoarse, so he cleared his throat. He said, 'Can you tell me about his dream? Please?'

Imogen's eyes shone. 'It's always the same. A man walks in the mountains. His hair sparkles white as frost. He wears a cloak of rich cloth that billows out around him. The cloak has real colours, rose-hip red and corn yellow, the sharp green of new beech leaves and the emerald green of mallard's feathers. Blue, too. The enamel blue of swallows' wings and fragile blue of harebells. There's marigold, cherry-blossom pink and chestnut brown.

'Luka says that he likes the man's hair. "It sparkles white," he says, "but it's not old man's hair, because he strides around with long legs. If he was an old man his legs would be all bent up and rickety."

'By the man's shoulder is an owl with eyes as big as carriage lamps and, by his feet, a hare with fur as fine as gossamer. Seven wolves wait at a distance, gaunt as grey ghosts. Their tongues loll and drip, but Luka says he isn't frightened of them, because he knows the man with the hair of frost is their master, and the wolves know it too.'

'I've never had dreams like that,' said Jez. 'My dreams are all about forgetting to put bread in the oven. Or having lead feet and not being able to run away from things.' He felt dumb beside his brother. He had no imagination.

'Luka's dream is so vivid!' cried Imogen. 'I love painting it. He says that the man swings down a bundle of twigs from his back. With a piece of iron and a pinch of tinder, he conjures up a spark and at once there is fire. The flames leap. The man's face shines gold. The hare and the wolves come near and the owl flies to a branch and softly stacks her wings. Other animals come out of the forest too – I've tried to draw them – a big bear and a wild boar with scimitar tusks. High in the sky there flies an eagle with golden eyes. A silver fish leaps up from the stream. And look! There's an otter slipping down the bank.

'Then the man puts his fingers in his mouth and

whistles. Down from the mountain bounds a great creature like a snow cloud. Its head is round and neat and its tail stretches behind it, as long as its body, and it has thick white fur dappled with dark rings. The creature winds itself around him as if it is a curl of mist winding round a mountain, and then Luka gets worried. He shouts out "Be careful! Look at its powerful big paws! It'll swipe you!"

'Instead, it purrs so deeply that the whole earth hums. It settles down by the fire, curls its tail around its head and goes to sleep.'

'Wow!' said Jez.

Imogen gave him a wide smile, then bit her lip. 'I know it sounds silly, but I wonder if Luka has gone looking for this dream world? It's so real to him. He knew exactly what the creature looked like. I think it's a leopard.' She pointed at the picture. 'There it is, look! The big cat.'

Jez stood up fast, knocking over the little chair, shouting, 'Of course!'

'Wait!' cried Imogen but Jez was already running out with the dog at his heels.

CHAPTER 9

BIG YELLOW EYES

If Luka dreamed about a big cat, thought Jez as he ran, was it the same as the cat in the notice on the chestnut tree? Or was it the wild beast, roaming around the village?

Jez stopped and stared up into the chestnut tree. The dog was watching it intently, one paw raised as if she was hunting, but Jez couldn't see what was up there. It must be the snow settling on the branches.

He hurried on to the bakery. Dimitri was collecting logs for the morning. He was sad. He had found the little blue body of a swallow by his woodshed door. It had returned expecting the spring, not this dead cold.

'Dimitri! Luka's not at home!' cried Jez.

'Hey, that's bad! I'll go and look for him.'

'But you've got to get up in a few hours' time. You need your sleep!'

'I won't sleep if I think Luka is out alone. Not with this wild beast on the prowl. And . . .' Dimitri stopped himself just in time. He had an awful feeling he already knew where Luka might be but he kept quiet. He did not want to worry Jez even more.

Tears welled in Jez's eyes. Dimitri would help, he always would!

'Thanks, Dimitri. If you check the village, I'll go up towards the mountains with the dog. I bet he's gone to the Depths of Lumb, because I told him not to.' Jez began to tremble. To hide his fear he stammered, 'Brrr, so cold and damp. Don't forget to close the woodshed door when you've finished. The last thing you want is wet wood to put the fires out,' and then he hurried home.

The house was cold as an empty coffin. He ran out into the yard. 'Luka? LUKA!' His voice ribboned away over the wall and up the hillside. No one answered.

He ran inside and rolled up a sleeping bag. He

grabbed a rucksack and searched out a torch, matches, a bundle of strong cord and a knife with a curved horn handle that had been his father's.

He paused, holding the knife in his left hand. With his right he stroked the ice-cold blade. He was trying to remember something. The knife stirred memories in the back of his mind as if it were a little spider sensing a twinge on the rope of silk linked to its web.

Jez packed his rucksack and pulled on extra clothes. Over everything he put his father's heavy brown jacket. It felt strange, to wear his father's clothes, but it felt warm and protecting too.

He stuffed apples deep into the corners of the rucksack and packed a lump of cheese, the scones and butter on top. He turned to go, and began to whistle a tune he'd heard often on the radio, a song about a blackbird singing in the night and then learning to fly.

The whistling died on his lips.

A pair of yellow eyes was watching him through the window. They blinked and vanished. Something fluttered away past the window.

At his side, the dog whimpered. Jez made himself

whistle again, like a kettle trying to boil. It helped a little.

Outside in the yard, the snow was mussed with tracks. Jez could not see them clearly because they had been disturbed and were already sprinkled with new snow. He thought he could see a print from Luka's boot. There were long marks, too, the tracks of a hare, and there were larger, rounder prints. They all led towards the hole in the wall. The stones glowed with tiny emerald forests of moss and copses of golden lichen. Jez had to bend down to get through the hole in the middle and the dog jumped through after him. The tracks led away on the other side, up to the trees.

At once a swarm of birds burst up from the branches, scarlet, yellow and gold in this dim light. They scattered into the sky as if someone had thrown up a handful of Christmas stars.

'Goldfinches!' cried Jez. 'It's a good omen! It means I'll find Luka!' For it was always Luka who heard the tinkling calls of the goldfinches first.

It was strange to walk up this hill without Luka touching his arm every few minutes to make sure he was still near. The world was silent. Jez saw just one light in the village below, bobbing through the streets like a glow-worm.

Dimitri. Maybe Imogen is right. I'm not on my own.

CHAPTER 10

THE CHOIR OF WOLVES

Dimitri the baker headed out of the village down the road towards the sea. On the way he knocked on doors and asked people to look out for Luka. Many people offered him a drink. So, warm with glassfuls of false courage, he trudged on until he came to a little wooden house with five sides. The roof sagged. Timbers stuck out of it like splinters. The windowpanes were cracked and thick with brown dirt, as if no human being had looked out of them for years, but Dimitri smelled wood smoke on the cold air. Vaskalia *was* there!

He rapped on the door, puffing breath into the

darkness like a small steam train. 'Come on, you inside! Open the door!'

At once the door creaked open.

Dimitri was a short man, but even he was taller than this woman wrapped up in shawls and scarves as if she was waiting inside a cocoon. She wore mittens of matted black stuff with her fingers poking out. Around her scrawny wrists were bangles of dull copper. Her eyes rolled at Dimitri. They looked in different directions. *She can see behind me!*

Her son Simlin hovered in the doorway behind her. Dimitri could see his pale face, his long hands and thin bare feet sticking out around her, as if together they were some strange god image. Vaskalia's wideness quite concealed her son's skinny body.

Dimitri cleared his throat and said, 'I'm looking for Luka. The boy who can't see properly.'

'I know perfectly well which boy you mean!' she snapped. 'I have seen him in all kinds of places.'

Dimitri could see a red eyeball of fire glowing in the middle of the floor behind the woman. Simlin went to crouch before it, chattering away to himself. Shapes hung from the beams, fluttering in the wind from the open door. They might have been dried fish, or posies of herbs and flowers, or spare scarves. The earthen floor was littered with white fragments of bone.

Dimitri's attention was drawn back to the woman who was muttering. She fluttered her stumpy eyelashes at him.

'Perhaps your son has seen the boy when he's been out, madame?' said Dimitri, taking a step backwards, thinking, Better be polite to a woman like this.

'We can't help you!' she said, and gnawed on her copper bangles.

'You heartless hag!' cried Dimitri before he could stop himself. 'People would help *you* if your son went missing!'

'My son *wouldn't* go missing, baker man. He never leaves my side, and I never go out, because there is a spell upon this house. If we go out, the spell will move in. And *you* are a fool to leave your bakery unattended. Who knows what evil might get in!'

'What superstitious old rubbish you talk, woman!' shouted Dimitri, thinking, And you are lying, too, you do go out, you sneak around my bakery!

'Take care what you say to me!' she shrieked. 'And take care out there! The wolves have returned to the forest. You'd make a tidy tea for them, baker man.' She put her head on one side and whispered, 'Listen . . . listen to the wolves singing.'

The moment she spoke of wolves, Dimitri heard them. Far away. One wolf howled. Then another. Soon there were three, each singing a slightly different note, howling in a mournful choir.

'A wolf choir sings of death,' crooned Vaskalia.

How could I have forgotten my shotgun on such a night? thought Dimitri.

She put her head on one side and looked coyly up at him. 'It's a bad winter, baker man. But it's not as bad as the winters *I* knew as a child. They can't take it these days. I rode to school on a billy goat with my inkwell tucked in my armpit to stop it freezing. My childhood was full of real hardship.'

'And you think mine wasn't?' said Dimitri. 'This winter is like no other. You know that!'

From under her scarves she took a little copper cup that glowed and held it out to him. A coy smile twitched her lips and she simpered, 'But I must make you welcome. Drink this to warm your bones.'

Dimitri hesitated. It's asking for trouble to refuse her hospitality. He raised the cup to his lips and knocked the liquid back. *Mmmm* . . . it was sweet and spicy, like nothing he had ever tasted before. The flavour crept around his throat and chest like fingers of fire.

'What is it?' he asked. 'It is delicious!'

'My very own recipe, baker man. I am so glad you like it.'

But then the coy flirt changed into a whirl of anger. 'Be off with you, fat man! And if you are wise – which you are not – you'll be more careful about the way you speak to me tomorrow.'

'Don't worry, I'm going!' roared Dimitri and he stormed away, muttering, 'Go boil your cauldron, crone!' and wishing he hadn't talked to her at all.

He made for the inn at the bend of the road, shining his torch straight ahead so that the beam bobbed across the snow like a will-o'-the-wisp.

But the inn wasn't as he remembered it. The top had been blown off and only the ground floor was left now.

Dimitri could see light behind the little windows. He heard the murmur of voices as he turned the big ring handle of the door.

At once lights dimmed and voices stopped. People had learned to dread the turning handle, the stranger at the door. Who would it be? An enemy or a friend? Men with garlands of bullets around their necks or someone bringing medicine for your child?

Dimitri peered into darkness. Bottles and glasses glinted in the light from the fire, but there was no one to be seen.

'I'm a friend! It's Dimitri from the bakery!' he called. People rose from behind the tables. The lamps were turned up high again and lit their faces softly as if they were in an old oil painting.

'Dimitri Founari!' cried the innkeeper. 'What brings you here on such a bad night? Not that I can remember a good one. The war has beheaded my inn and the winter has turned my brandy into syrup!'

'That's a tragedy! I'm looking for the boy Luka. He's gone missing.'

'Is that the odd one? Jez's little brother?'

'That's him,' said Dimitri. He turned and called out, 'Please, keep your eyes open, everyone. He might be sleeping in your barn, or fallen down somewhere and broken his ankle.'

The innkeeper filled a glass for Dimitri. 'No need to pay,' he said, holding up his hand against the coins Dimitri offered. 'It's good to see you, even if it was trouble that brought you here. Please sit down, Dimitri.'

Dimitri did so, thankfully. He felt shaken up. That doll woman had unnerved him. Maybe he would not leave immediately. He tipped back his glass and the warmth spread across his throat. He glanced round. There were faces he recognised but had not seen for months. There was George the shoemaker, Peter who drove the rusty village bus and that old doctor with the straggly white hair.

A voice spoke from near the fire. 'There's a wild cat on the loose. You men should hunt it down.'

'Oh, our forest is still full of beasts,' said the innkeeper, polishing a glass. 'But they keep well out of the way because of the war.'

'Maybe you should do something about them,'

growled the voice. It sounded like the toes of a boot swirling patterns in gravel. Dimitri had now had so many drinks that he could just make out three blurred figures sitting in the nook of the fireplace. He saw snowboots and hooded faces lined with fur. He saw something else too. The leather sheath at the man's waist. That must be a big knife.

He swigged the burning liquid in his glass and said, 'We've always lived alongside the wild creatures.'

'You men should hunt them. Kill them before they kill you. Think of the fur. Think of the money you could make, selling pelts!'

At the mention of money, there was a murmuring of assent through the inn. Dimitri didn't like it. His father and his grandfather had only killed when they needed food. No killing for killing's sake. If times were hard they killed bears. He stood up unsteadily and blinked at the men in the inn, the villagers he knew. Their twisted faces swam before him. Their eyes were shining at the thought of a hunt. He sighed. There had been too much shooting and killing these last few years, not enough food or money or comfort.

Dimitri drained his glass, feeling the liquid burst hot in his chest, then saw a violin case on a table. He had not played it for years. His own fiddle lay high on a shelf at the bakery, covered in dust. There were no longer weddings or parties or dancing days. There were only wakes, when everyone wailed or tore their hair with grief. And now Luka had disappeared. Dimitri wanted to weep, because he loved Luka and Jez as if they were his own sons, and they had suffered so much already.

He wandered across and opened the case. He picked up the fiddle and placed it on his shoulder. Taking the bow, he played music that was full of the sadness that had happened in the land.

'What's that tune called, baker?' asked an old man, wiping his eyes.

'I don't know what it's called. I just know the music from a long time ago,' said Dimitri. 'The old tunes are the best.'

But this one was just too sad. He put down the violin, a little unsteadily. He was beginning to feel unwell. It was not just the drink; he must have caught some illness. His head hurt. He felt dizzy. He lurched off towards the door.

The strangers in the fireplace leaned forward to watch him go.

CHAPTER 11

GARLIC AND WET NELLIE

Dimitri knew he should continue to look for Luka, but he felt too ill and his feet led him home. When he reached the bakery, he staggered straight upstairs to bed and fell asleep at once, still in his boots and greatcoat. He had wild, terrifying dreams of being chased by a shrieking, spitting troll with a scarf around its head.

He woke up in a house that was hotter than he had ever known it. *Hot as hell.* Dimitri went slowly downstairs. He had a bad, bad feeling.

His baker's instinct sent him to look at the last of his yeast, the baker's miracle.

Dimitri sighed like a furnace. It had turned to brown sludge and the miller would not be able to deliver again in this snow.

He went into his larder, lowered his face to the big white jug and sniffed. The milk smelled like dead fish. Dimitri felt his stomach heave. How could it have turned so quickly? Stone walls and the stone floor kept the larder cool, always.

What about the butter? Big Katrin used it to bake her cakes every third day, when the bread was finished. Dimitri fetched the three-legged stool. He climbed on to it, swaying with dizziness. The butter was slumped across the white marble slab. It began to drip down on to the floor and set into a greasy yellow pool.

'It's like candle wax,' groaned Dimitri. Teetering on the stool, he stuck his finger into the sludge and raised it to his lips.

'Eugh! Rancid!' he spat.

The handle of the street door turned. Dimitri jumped down off the stool and crouched on the floor with his arms wrapped around his head like a little child. He heard her boots stamp on the mat, one! two!

Pause . . . Dimitri turned his head beneath his arms and opened one eye. He could just see her standing in her coat. Her nose wrinkled. Dimitri stood up and watched her round the larder door. She untied her scarf and laid it carefully on the table.

Dimitri took a deep breath and trotted out of the larder.

'Oh. Hello, Katrin. The – er – yeast . . . milk . . . and butter . . .' He felt like a naughty little boy at school, telling tales to the teacher. He hurried to show Big Katrin the sludgy crumbs that would never raise the bread.

Katrin sniffed at the curdled milk. Then she opened a window, took the jug and poured the whole smelly lot on to the snow outside. SPLOOSH SPLATTER!

She headed for her butter. Dimitri ran after her and hopped up on to his stool so that his eyes were on a level with hers. Katrin's eyes reminded Dimitri of the dark brown sugar and cinnamon mix he sprinkled thickly on buns so that it melted into dark caramel.

Then he remembered. Vaskalia. What had she given him to drink? He could not remember. But now he felt ill. The hairs on the back of his neck rose, and into his mind crowded old enemies, family feuds and ancient malice. He thought of lies, bad wishes, pins stuck into dolls, necks and curses hissed in corners.

Dimitri babbled away to Big Katrin, all about the cottage with five sides and the dead fish and bones and leaves, and Simlin crouched by the fire.

'Katrin, she talked of spoiling and poison and she says she's seen Luka in all kinds of places . . .'

Big Katrin looked at him for a long moment. She took a cloth and poured the rancid butter on to it, knotting the top. She wiped down the marble slab. She fished out the useless blob of yeast and wrapped it up in muslin.

Big Katrin cut thick slices of Wet Nellie – bread pudding, very rich and sweet, made from any bread that was left over at the end of the day. She selected a ginger cake shaped like a bar of bronze, a golden cake studded with cherries, and a cake as thickly embroidered with nuts as the centre of a sunflower. From the back of a cupboard she pulled out folded cardboard and assembled a large box. She set her chosen cakes in the box and packed the gaps with slices of Wet Nellie.

'Eh? What's all that lot for?' cried Dimitri. 'Where's your pride, Katrin?'

Katrin put on her scarf again and tied it under her chin. All the while she gazed at Dimitri. He let himself have a little gaze back. Those eyes could turn a man into a blancmange!

'Wait! I'll come with you, Katrin,' he cried. 'I know exactly what to do!'

He ran into his larder and reached under the shelf where he kept a basket of vegetables. He rummaged around until his hand closed round a bulb that felt as if it was wrapped in tissue paper. Garlic. A fat, juicy bulb made of pink and white cloves wrapped in their papery skins.

Dimitri waved it at Katrin. He hesitated. Then he opened his mouth wide, shoved the whole bulb in and bit it. *Garlic!* THAT was how to deal with curses, vampires and old magic. Dimitri spluttered and coughed. His eyes and nose streamed until he had to turn away from Katrin and spit the whole chewed bulb on to the floor.

Katrin looked at him. She waved her hand in front

of her nose and pulled a face. She handed him a small piece of Wet Nellie to dull the burning taste of garlic in his mouth.

Then she closed the cake box again and waited for Dimitri to open the door.

CHAPTER 12

THE DEPTHS OF LUMB

Luka fell down into the Depths of Lumb, clutching and scrabbling, trying to stop, but everything he clutched fell with him, in a hailstorm of stones and rattling scree.

He struggled to sit up. His back was hurting. His body stung. There was something encasing him and it was heavy. He could not get his breath properly. There was weight all round his face, cold weight. He stuck out his tongue and tasted snow. *Idiot. Idiot!*

Luka set his mind's eye on the Cloud Cat. It was leaping across a mountain chasm. Luka thought of its grace and power and at once his spirits lifted. Strength flowed down his arms and legs. He began to dig with his hands. He pushed and pushed with his right shoulder, digging and shoving, although his arms were weak. With a strange creak, the snow on his right side split and crumbled and fell away. Luka crawled out from the drift. He sat there, numb.

He had lost sight of the Cloud Cat and it was gone again.

He began to feel hot. He pulled off his hat, and then he heard it. Under the earth. First it was a long vibration, as if Dimitri had plucked one of his low fiddle strings. Then it rumbled and grumbled. Something was stirring, down under the ground.

It grew louder and louder until Luka had to clap his hands over his ears. The noise was like the roaring of those enormous tanks that had rolled and bumped through the village, with lots of different noises too, grinding and groaning, screaming and shuddering. Luka heard flopping and slithering and knew that something vast was shifting around underneath him.

It's a tangle of serpents, in a great big glistening knot, rolling nearer and nearer!

The noise was right below him now. It was slithering up to the crust of the world. Everything was heating up and there was a horrible stench that made him cough and try to pinch his nose. It was the smell of something rotting.

Luka remembered what Imogen said whenever he was feeling bad: 'The only way is up.' Summoning every tiny drop of his energy, Luka clawed his way upwards away from whatever was coming after him. Something tried to grab his ankle and pull him down. *The only way is up!*

CHAPTER 13

THE GHOST IN THE TREE

Jez and the dog went backwards and forwards, forwards and backwards in the snow, trying to follow Luka's footprints.

The dog barked hysterically at the same unknown scent she had smelled out in the yard the night before, the scent of danger.

And there were other smells. Some of them she could eat! The dog lolloped ahead, nose in the snow. She stopped suddenly with one ear pricked and the other flopped over like the flap of an envelope. There was something ahead, just for her, something moving. It had long, black-tipped ears.

The dog chased after it, over the hilltop and out of sight.

'Dog! Get back here at once!' hollered Jez. He called and whistled and cursed her, but she would not come back. *Everything leaves me. Even the dog.*

He caught his foot on a root and sank down in the snow, blinking back angry tears. He wiped his face on his sleeve and swore some more. Stop snivelling. Pull yourself together. You've had worse happen than a dog running away from you. Think what you'd look like if Imogen saw you! Awful! All red-eyed and snotty. Jez gulped and swallowed and took charge of his breathing. It slowed down. The tears stopped.

All right. I'm going to find you, Luka, and nothing will stop me.

Jez stood up. He breathed deep and stretched tall, and set off up the hillside towards the Depths of Lumb where he felt sure Luka had gone. He wore his father's coat and his mother's old hat as if they were armour. He'd had to work hard to keep going without his parents. The world was such a vicious place. Stupid Luka did not realise what a dangerous thing he was doing. We don't need to go looking for adventure, Luka. We have enough real danger.

A grey shape caught his eye. Its flight was slanted and silent. A ghost! He dared not turn round to look at it. All of a sudden it flew ahead of him. It soared up to the top of the hill, and then back again, almost as if it wanted to be seen.

Go away, please go away! But it didn't. It swooped past again and landed in a tree ahead. It paused. Then came a loud SHRIEK! Jez almost jumped out of his skin. The grey shape shrieked again. Trembling, he made himself face it. Yellow eyes glared at him as if he was the only thing alive in the world.

It's just an owl, Jez realised. He gave it a jaunty wave and set off on his way, but the owl flew across his path and landed on the first tree again. And then it growled.

'GET LOST, OWL!' Jez shouted, and beat his hands together. Why couldn't it leave him alone? He tried to walk east, muttering and swearing away, but in spite of himself his legs changed direction. He tramped towards the owl, the only living thing in the snowy world, a big feathery bundle of hope in the emptiness. The owl shrieked with triumph. Its voice boomed through the silent night like the foghorn of a liner in the ocean. It launched itself into the air and Jez followed.

And then began the worst snowstorm Jez had ever seen. It began quickly, a whirlwind of white flakes. There was nothing but snow between the earth and the sky. Jez felt as if he was spinning in the centre of a white top. The thicker it became, the darker it seemed. As Jez blinked up, the flakes looked like big pieces of soot. They stung his face with cold.

Everything disappeared, everything but snow. It changed the landscape until it was all the same. Jez felt smothered in it, snow in his eyes and nostrils and mouth. His lungs sighed with pain every time he breathed in, but his face was numb now and he could no longer feel the snowflakes stinging his skin. He could see nothing, no owl, no trees, no tracks, and he realised with dismay that the little space left by the snow was growing dark.

Jez lurched on through the blizzard, smack into something hard. It felt like a stone wall. Surely nobody could live out here? Keeping his shoulder against the wall, he edged along. At once he turned a corner and fell in through a doorway. It was a tiny place, but Jez's heart leaped with hope. Shelter! There was snow on the floor and some wet hay, too. And a little fireplace. And a small, high window space without any glass. Jez sank down on to his knees. It must be a hut for goatherds.

Relief flooded through him like a hot drink. After his heart had slowed down, he struggled to his feet and pulled the door towards him, dragging it over thick snow. He would stay here until it grew light. He would sleep. He would set out again at dawn tomorrow, rested and full of energy.

When Jez woke, it was dark. He did not know whether it was night or morning. So much snow had fallen that it was pressed right up against the window space, hard as concrete. Not one chink of light or air could get through. Jez threw himself at the door, but it would not budge. He was snowed in.

CHAPTER 14

CUT

Luka struggled to get his breath. Two things were fighting, pulling him between them in different directions, like starving dogs with a piece of meat. He set his mind on keeping himself in one piece.

He had to keep climbing. Twice he slipped down again, not far but enough to make him cry with frustration. And then his eyelids turned blinding white. Daylight. The world had opened out to the sky again. He heard a little bleating noise. Something jumped away across the snow-covered rocks. It must be a mountain goat, up on the crags.

Luka's throat hurt as if he'd been shouting too much,

but he thought exultantly, Jez, I'm free! Free from the Depths of Lumb.

Luka sat up and pulled his backpack on to his knee. He slipped the straps over his shoulders and then he took out his drum. He tapped it gently. Look, no gloves. What had he done with them? His hands hurt from the climb upwards, yet his fingers were warm and full of energy.

He began to play a soft rhythm, tapping with his fingertips. The sound was soothing, rather like a lullaby, except that it didn't send him to sleep. It slowed his breathing down and made him feel very calm. He set his mind on the Cloud Cat again. There it was, in the far distance, leaping down the crags towards him on its powerful paws. He saw the eyes, set like pieces of cold gold in its face, and watched its shoulder blades slide like pistons under its dappled coat. *Please come nearer. Please come to me*.

The Cloud Cat stayed where he could see it, but just out of his reach. Concentrating on it drained his strength. *Come HERE!* he whined, near to tears. But try as he might, he could not coax it any closer. Would he ever bring it near enough?

As Luka sat so far away, playing his drum, a hungry rat scuttled towards the rope bridge. It crawled on to the logs at the beginning of the bridge and began to gnaw at the rope.

The rope gave up and broke and the bridge snaked away across the chasm with the rat clinging on tight. The bridge dangled down uselessly from the other side of the gorge, but the rat scrambled all the way to the top as if it was boarding a ship, and scuttled away to a new life.

CHAPTER 15

THE WOLVES AT THE DOOR

'Damn you, Luka!' shouted Jez. 'Why did you have to run away? Why couldn't you be satisfied with just being alive?' He kicked the door again and again, in a solid, angry rhythm. 'I came in here to shelter from the weather and now I can't get out again. I'll suffocate and starve! I'll be trapped in here until . . .'

When the sounds began, Jez thought at first that they were coming from some awful place far inside himself. Somewhere he had never known. Eerie, sad sounds. Hungry sounds. He shook his head and concentrated. They weren't very far away. Wolves! They were coming nearer. They must have heard him kicking and shouting.

What a fool he was! He backed away from the door, waiting. The howling came closer, until he knew they were right outside the hut. Then it stopped. There was sniffing. Jez closed his eyes but against his eyelids he saw sharp snouts, dripping red tongues, scimitar teeth. And then there was one sharp bark. That was no wolf. That was the damned dog!

Silence. Then another sound began, worse than the howling. Scrabbling in the snow. Digging. They were digging him out, digging at the snow against the door. What would happen when they'd shifted it? Jez looked wildly around him, for something to barricade himself in. But the door opened outwards. Wolves could not open it. Jez had a moment of relief until he pictured them, slavering and sniffing, waiting for him to emerge. He would never get away.

Jez was shaking with fear. He felt like a piece of meat waiting in a deep freeze. The noise changed place. They were outside the window. The digging was steady, deliberate. A wolf could squeeze in through that space. How would he deal with it? How many were there? They would squeeze in, one at a time, to get him!

The digging stopped. Why? What had they heard? Silence. Then Jez heard it, far away, the whine of a rifle. A flurry, and he knew the wolves were gone. Had the dog followed them? What a traitress she was!

He pushed at the snow in the blocked window. The digging wolves had dislodged it. Desperately Jez hit at it, scooping snow down inside, all over his feet.

Snow crumbled in the top corner. A chink of grey light! Jez threw himself at the window, scrabbling and sobbing, until he had pulled down a space. He pushed his way through, gasping for air and light and freedom.

Out again in the emptiness, he saw the snow scuffed with the tracks of his saviours, yet the wolves and the dog were nowhere to be seen. The sky was still sullen. Snow smoked the air. Through it Jez glimpsed a small tree. On it sat the owl, waiting for him, ready to continue on their journey.

CHAPTER 16

WAR TRUCK

The owl stretched up on its branch, spread its wings and flew due north, towards the mountains. This was the wrong way, surely, yet Jez's feet followed, as if something magnetic in the earth was leading them on.

The further north he went, the deeper lay the snow. He lost his balance once and found himself waist-deep in a drift. Heaving himself out of it was exhausting. His footsteps became slower and heavier because his boots were soaking wet.

'Wait, owl!' he shouted. It settled in a tree and stacked its wings, turning towards him a disgruntled face, as if to say, *I shouldn't be up in the daytime. I should be asleep with my head swivelled right away from distractions such as you.*

Jez took out one of Big Katrin's scones. It tasted rich and sweet. He chewed the sultanas while his mind churned with worries. *How long do you think you can survive in this wilderness, Luka?*

Jez knew that if he kept his mind and hands busy, he would be all right. He could get water from melted snow. He had food. He had matches for a fire. *I know! I shall make myself some snowshoes!*

He scrambled over to a birch tree and peeled off two wide strips of silvery bark. In his rucksack was the ball of strong cord, which he used to bind the bark on to his boots, under his feet and round the heel. Jez stood up in the snowshoes. He took careful steps. They slid across the snow like silk.

The hill was becoming steeper. Jez turned to look back. He could just see the village, far below. The roofs that remained were gathered on the slopes like a flock of white birds and beyond them he could even see the sea, ice grey and rilled with silver. The road that led out of the village was visible from here, outlined by faint verges in the snow. That road was the last place Jez had seen his mother. She had been taken away in the back of a truck. Jez had watched, helpless, from the upstairs window, with Luka clinging to his knees.

Whenever Jez turned to that road he saw his mother again, looking back at them, her face just a pale star in the darkness of the truck. He felt as if someone was reaching inside his chest and wringing out his heart hard with both hands, as if it was a piece of washing. *Luka, I'm all you've got now, like it or lump it.*

The snowlight up here was dazzling. It hurt Jez's eyes so he couldn't see properly. Right! He peeled off more bark from a branch, like skin peeling off a leg, took out his father's knife with the curved handle and cut a mask to shield his eyes from the glare. He made a hole in each side, threaded through a length of cord and tied it round his head.

Snow specs! At least I won't get snow-blind.

Then Jez heard an engine.

The noise was far away. It was the engine of something heavy, inching its way through the snow. Where could he hide? He flung himself to the ground;

by the time whatever it was reached him, he would be covered by falling snow, invisible in the wasteland of white.

He turned his face to the side. There it was. A grey vehicle, a war truck, with huge wheels covered in caterpillar tracks, grinding towards him.

Voices. Jez saw heads in the open back of the vehicle. There were helmets, dark, bulbous, netted so that they reminded him of the eyes of houseflies. The ground shook under the heavy armoured truck, shuddering under his body.

It's going to run me over!

CHAPTER 17

OLD MAGIC

Big Katrin stood before the little house with five sides. Black smoke belched from the stovepipe chimney in the centre of the roof. Katrin banged three times on the door and the whole house shook. Lumps of snow slid off the roof and plopped to the ground.

She banged on the door again. It creaked open. Katrin saw Simlin's pallid face. He stared straight at her without blinking. Big Katrin had always won staring competitions when she was a child, and she could still win. Soon Simlin cast his eyes down to his thin bare feet. Big Katrin heard springs twang and a dull thud as Vaskalia flopped off the bed. She heard the shuffle of small feet towards the door. Vaskalia peered round her son's waist and her face shrivelled with malice.

'How's your bread his morning, ogress?' she taunted.

Big Katrin ducked her head and strode in through the door. Something crunched under her scarlet boots. Katrin's nose wrinkled. The cottage smelled of old flesh, unwashed clothes and some other things that should not be in anyone's house. Katrin set her cake box down on the greasy table. She noticed something glinting in the firelight. It was the blade of a big cleaver.

Vaskalia licked her lips with a dark pointed tongue.

'My, oh my . . . you've brought me a wedding cake!' she simpered.

Katrin put the bundles of bad yeast and butter on the table. At once Vaskalia screamed with laughter and her eyes swivelled and rolled like the eyes of a chameleon. She shrieked and said, 'So you think *I* made the bakery red hot? You think *I* turned your butter and yeast so foul and rancid? Am I so powerful? Well, you're right! I did, I did!'

Big Katrin opened the box. Vaskalia began to dribble. She gloated, 'Hee hee! Cakey cake! I accept your offering, ogress, and I accept your apology. I shall not turn your yeast bad again.'

Big Katrin inclined her head graciously. Vaskalia and her son immediately crammed their mouths full of cake.

'But let it be a warning to you!' spluttered Vaskalia, with cake flying from her mouth. She chomped on for a few minutes and then she turned an eye on Katrin and hissed, 'Never forget the old magic. This war has brought forgetting. Soldiers from across the sea bring new magic. They bring trinkets, pictures that move, needles to stick in sick people, boxes that steal your face away. When the soldiers leave, they take their magic with them, but the old magic is still here around us. It always will be. So you should keep that blind boy indoors!'

A lump of spit full of crumbs landed on Katrin's chin. Katrin took out her handkerchief and wiped her face carefully, thinking, There will be a spot there in the morning. She saw Vaskalia's tongue dart around her lips, flipping any crumbs it found back into her mouth. Katrin took a step back, out of range.

Something hit the door. Vaskalia scuttled across the room and opened it.

At first Katrin thought the creature was some giant beetle, because it wore a carapace of long wings, but it had only two legs, not six. The two legs were strong and scaly and its feet bore thick talons. Its head was bald. It glared at Big Katrin with eyes as unchanging as stones. Those legs could pick up a child.

The big bird waddled up to Vaskalia, opened its beak and dropped a bloodied rabbit at her feet. It turned its head towards Katrin and stared at her. Opening its dark wings, it beat them so hard that gusts of icy air drove the flames in the fire flat.

Vaskalia said, 'Why don't you ask my Bone Cracker if he's seen your blind boy?'

Big Katrin thought, Why does Vaskalia hate Luka so?

The instant this question came into Katrin's mind, Vaskalia scuttled underneath a high shelf. Katrin saw grey figures up there, small dolls, like mummies swaddled in dirty bandages, stuck as full of pins as porcupines. Vaskalia reached up and felt around. Her hand could not find what it was groping for, but Big Katrin was across the room with one stride and found it first in a nest of sticky cobwebs. She picked it up and held it, just out of reach.

Vaskalia squealed with rage and jumped up and down, battering Katrin with her black-mittened fists. She sank her teeth into Katrin's arm and hung on tight, little feet kicking in the air, but Katrin shook her off as a terrier shakes a rat.

She looked down at what lay cupped in her hands.

It was a ball made of glass, like the float for a sea fisherman's net. The glass was smeared with grease and soot. Katrin turned it over and caught her breath. Inside it was Luka.

He was struggling with something inside the glass ball. His arms were beating. Then he stopped moving and curled up tight, hiding his face.

Vaskalia hissed, 'What do you see? Break your silence, you stubborn ogress!'

She picked up the cleaver, still watching Katrin. The blade glinted in the firelight. On the table lay a piece of stone, strewn with leaves, clusters of purple berries and curls of bark. The stone was the colour of pewter. Katrin stilled her mind. She knew that she must not give away any secret about Luka because this woman would use it against him.

Vaskalia began to chop, with a hand at each end of the cleaver. The blade was as deadly as the blade on a guillotine. The purple berries bled on to the stone. A bone fell from the rafters above, and Vaskalia could not stop chopping so she chopped that too, slicing it all into smaller and smaller shreds, as her eyes swivelled. The mixture smelled like bad cheese. Vaskalia murmured, 'Every precious ingredient is from my garden, except the gift from my faithful Bone Cracker. I have more than a hundred plants out there.'

She's making old magic. Why? What does she want with Luka?

At once Vaskalia knew Katrin's thought. She hissed, 'I'll tell you this, ogress, because I know you will stay silent. In Jez and Luka's family there waits a gift. It comes to every fifth generation. Their great-great-grandfather had the gift. A child of each fifth generation has the gift. That child must be strong enough to carry a great burden on his shoulders. The only children are Luka and that foolish Jez! Ha!' Vaskalia spat into a little cup on the table. 'Jez? That lanky great scarecrow has no gift for anything, so it must be Luka's gift. But it should be *my* son's turn, *Simlin*'s turn! It should be my family that gets that gift!'

Before Katrin's horrified eyes, Vaskalia whirled the cleaver above her head, faster and faster, crying 'Luka's father should have married *me*! Think what a magnificent pair we would have made! What powerful children we would have brought howling into the world! But the fool married HER when he could have had ME! I cannot bring myself to speak her name!' Vaskalia filled her cheeks with spittle and spat hard into the fire, and the flames exploded and roared up, emerald green.

'Just LOOK at the droolgob I got instead!' She hurled the cleaver hard at her son. It missed him by a hair's breadth and stuck into the wall, quivering with a long, high note. 'Look at him! What a mooncalf and a milksop he is!'

Simlin whimpered in the corner. Poor sallow creature, thought Big Katrin. For the first time she noticed a red birthmark on his forehead. It was shaped like a scorpion, with its stinging tail twisted up over its back.

Vaskalia's eyes spun and threatened to pop out of

their sockets and roll across the floor. She growled, 'I'm telling you, Katrin, that Luka does not know he has a gift, not yet. If he discovers his gift and uses it, just once, it will go from strength to strength. He will have it forever and all our lives will change. For better or for worse, I cannot say! And *I* have something that belongs with that gift. Something Luka will kill for!'

What is it? Katrin put her head on one side. *And where is it?*

'Ha! You'll not trick me into telling you that!' cried Vaskalia. 'It is hidden in the most secret place of all. It will only be given if I wish it!'

Big Katrin glanced down at the ball cupped in her hands and raised her eyebrows. Vaskalia's eyes levelled and both looked at Katrin. *She's looking straight at me so she must be lying.*

'My family has used that seeing ball for hundreds of years,' she said. 'We are not ordinary village peasants like you common folk here. I can see Luka, wherever he is!'

We must find Luka before she does, vowed Katrin.

She set the ball carefully back up on the shelf.

Vaskalia hissed, 'Just as well you take such care,

ogress. That tells me you see the blind boy in there. Listen; if the seeing ball is broken, whoever is in it will die!'

Big Katrin hurried back through the village to the bakery. A notice hung on the door. It was a bit of brown cardboard from a box, fixed on by two nails, and written in thick pencil.

NO BRED TWODAY BICOS OF BAD BAD SIRKUMSTANSEES SORRY

Katrin sighed with sadness but her spirits lifted when she smelled coffee brewing. Dimitri would have made a pot of strong coffee to calm him down. Katrin needed some too, after her time with that woman. Together they must plan how to get the boys back.

CHAPTER 18

SHIFT

Luka heard something he had not heard for weeks. Gunfire.

One, two, three, four rifle shots, tearing through the air, one after another, far away. Not near enough to hurt *him*, but they would hurt someone all right, kill someone. The war was still going on, in fits and fatal starts.

'Please stay at home, Jez. Please stay safe!' he pleaded.

After the gunfire stopped, Luka listened to the silence. But into the silence crept the whispering. Once again he heard those words inside his head. *Idiot. Saphead. Moonraker. My mother knows all about you. She knows who you really are. Idiot!*

When the words began, Luka felt small and helpless. The whispering always made him feel as if he was shrinking, but now the shrinking feeling turned into anger. He would *not* have these words inside his head! Why couldn't the Whisperer just shut up and stop picking on him? Luka cried, 'So your mother knows all about me, does she, Mr Whisperer? She knows who I really am, does she?'

He stood up and waved his arms above his head, shouting, 'Well, *I'll* show you who I really am! *I'll* show you what I can become! All of you!'

He stamped his feet in the snow, turned round and round like a spinning top, and fell down again, giggling helplessly. When the giggling stopped, Luka sat up straight. He felt calm and sure now. The anger had ebbed away. It left behind it determination, cold and hard as iron.

Luka cleared his throat. He settled down to play the drum once more. He sat drumming softly, in time to the beat of his heart. This time he would not stop. His spirit lifted. Sweat broke out all over his face and body.

And suddenly the Cloud Cat was near him. Luka

could reach out his hand and touch that luxuriant white fur. He stroked it! The fur was dense and dappled with dark rings, as if drops of melted snow had fallen from trees and patterned the snow below. He saw its head just higher than his own, felt its hot breath on his cheek. The cat was panting slightly. Luka gazed up at its rounded head with the small ears, the long powerful body and thick scarf tail, and realised that he was not seeing with his mind's eye now.

The Cloud Cat had come to him at last.

It made him want to get to his feet and dance! It made him want to leap into the light. His life was a cage, and the Cloud Cat had come to help him escape from it. Currents of warm energy ran between them. *Take me with you, wherever you are going, Cloud Cat! Let me be you, and see through your eyes.*

He stopped drumming. He sat quite still. The cat filled his mind. He smelled its hot, sour breath and saw its curved teeth. He heard a rattling sound from its throat. He smiled as he looked into its gold nugget eyes and felt them drink him in until he forgot himself. The cat was all around him, left and right, front and back.

Luka let go of himself. It was as if he let himself step off a mountainside into emptiness. He was lost, happily lost, and it didn't hurt at all.

Luka's heart stopped. He was not breathing. He knew he was drifting, shifting through things he should have felt, but didn't.

The whole world stepped sideways to let him go. Luka left his body and was with the Cloud Cat at last.

They were running along a twisting path; Luka's eyes were wide open, seeing straight ahead. Luka felt strong shoulders rocking beneath dense fur and round paws padding on snow. He heard deep, fast breathing somewhere near, and saw that it was getting lighter because they were climbing, away from the Depths, up rocks so steep that Luka almost felt upside down, but quite safe.

He had a picture in his mind, a picture that moved: a boy the same as himself sitting on a great white leopard, riding on it as if he was a jockey on a horse. The boy's arms were wrapped round its strong neck, his fingers plunged among the charcoal roses on its fur.

Luka felt his breathing begin again, but it was very quick and light. He watched a cloud of crystals drift as he breathed out. His shower of crystal breath fell on to the snow crust with a soft, rustling sound. So *that's* what that sound had been!

And Luka could see. Away from them stretched dazzling ranges of blue sky and white mountainside. Below spread forests, laden with snow. Among the trees darted small animals, busy in their lives. The world was brilliant with colour. In the rivers he glimpsed the silver gleam of fishes and the bright-eyed faces of water animals with sleek brown bodies.

High up here on the mountainside, he heard the wind tear around the peaks, singing its wild song, free in a landscape without people. It brought him the cold salt smell of the sea. Luka could see it through long-sighted eyes, way down in the distance, the sea of silver and violet, moving and staying still.

And then they sprang in a high arc without breathing, over the dark place, over torrents of foaming water, and landed, only to leap and bound away over rocks frozen white as pearls. Luka wanted to roar with the freedom. No gunshot, no people, no fighting!

Padding feet along snow, warm feet covered with fur, not breaking the snow crust, then along rock as smooth as a frozen lake, silver and blue, loping assuredly, so high they must be up in heaven! Into darkness, but a friendly dark. Not sightless. Dry. No cutting wind now.

Hot, rough tongue scrubbing his face clean. Lie down, tummy very hungry, into a bag with food, eat, *chuff chuff*! Look up at dark blue spangled with stars. Purr with pleasure. So tired. So restful now. Out of danger. Safe. Safe enough to sleep at last.

All around was deep darkness. Real darkness, not the shades and creeping shadows he had become used to over the past few years. This was deep and comforting as velvet. There were little galleries lined with black velvet too, honeycombing off the big cave.

Luka lay warm and content on a wide ledge. He had the strength to do almost anything.

Again he felt light, quick breathing. Was it his? Was he breathing with someone else? There was a rhythm, as if he was playing his drum light and fast. But he wasn't. He listened and realised that there were two other, lighter beats, like a pair of tiny tabla. He thought they were in him and all around him, part of him.

The velvet cave was full of a strong cat smell. Like lots of Syrups and her kittens, but fiercer.

There was another smell in this cave, too. It was the scent of burning wood, as if someone was making charcoal, as they did deep in the forest. Luka heard the crackling and sparking of twigs. The walls of the cave glowed orange. A huge shadow spread across the orange wall. It was the shadow of a great cat, towering over him. It turned its round face down towards Luka and curled back its lips in a soft snarl. A smaller shadow appeared on the wall. It was the shadow of a boy, curled up on the ledge, and the cat put down its head and nuzzled the boy.

Echoes began to travel softly all around the cave and in and out of the smaller caves, running around the honeycomb and back again as if the cave was a whispering gallery. Words. The words echoed each other over and over again, catching each other up, like dominoes. They were dream words that mesmerised Luka, more like music than language, but they were words meant just for him. Luka understood what they said.

'You chose the most difficult shift first, Luka. Reckless boy! The hare came to you and waited. The owl came too. They would be simple companions for your first change, but oh no! Luka aims high. Luka wants the Cloud Cat to come down from the mountain top, he wants to shift into her splendour! She is a willing spirit, a companion for your wonder, yes, but she cannot stay with you for long, not this time. You are too selfish. You have not considered her life, her needs, or what danger you put her in. You must learn caution, Luka, and patience too. These qualities you need to fulfil yourself. I wonder if you will remember that next time . . .'

The great cat shadow stirred on the orange wall. It flowed across the cave and drew the boy shadow inside itself.

CHAPTER 19

OWL SHRIEK

Jez lay motionless in the snow, long after the ground had stopped shuddering. Snow fell and settled on his body while the wheels of the war truck ground away, carrying its faceless soldiers and their guns somewhere else.

Silence.

At last his body stirred. Jez struggled up on to his hands and knees and tried to stretch his aching limbs. He shook off his snow cover. That was a close call.

The moon shone on the snow slope and turned it into liquid silver. The owl fluttered ahead of Jez, as softly as a giant moth. It landed again and turned to glare at him. Now he heard water hurrying past and saw that the owl seemed to be standing in a stream. The water raced, dark as mercury. This must be the source of the river that flowed past the village and on to the sea. Jez saw stepping stones across the stream. He counted seven. The owl was perched on the middle stone, as still as an ornament on a mantelpiece.

It took off again, leading Jez over the stream and up to a mountain ledge that gleamed in the moonlight. A large rock jutted out above it like a canopy, keeping out the worst of the weather.

Jez sank down on to the ledge under the rock canopy. He was exhausted. He took out his sleeping bag and burrowed into it. His body felt heavy and lumpy with tiredness. It just wanted to give up. Just as he was about to drop off to sleep, there was an explosion in the distance, a dull boom. Then silence. It must have been a landmine, or a bomb. *Boom*. Then there was the crack and whine of a rifle shot. Jez felt as if these sounds had been with him all his life. In the far distance he thought he saw an orange glow as if something had been set alight.

Jez's body craved sleep. But his mind drifted. He saw

his father's dear face as he crouched by the house wall, looking at Jez, mouthing, *Stay over there! Don't come near* . . . and then the vicious, deadly whine of rifle fire, and then . . .

Jez's dream moved away from that unbearable image. It struggled to a cold ledge in the mountains. In this dream there was a big grey owl. The owl fluttered around as if it was uncertain whether or not to settle. Finally it perched on his rucksack. Jez did not know whether it slept or kept watch because he fell into a deep sleep, as if he might not wake up for days.

He was enveloped by a different nightmare, as suffocating as if someone had put a pillow over his face. In the nightmare he heard a cracking sound, over and over again. A big, dark kite with a white face painted on it was hovering above him, but it was a kite without a string. Something alive was dangling helplessly underneath it. Jez did not know what it was. Something small. Twist and moan as he might, Jez just could not wake himself up.

CHAPTER 20

SPLINTERS AND BONES

Vaskalia had been busy all evening, sticking pins into her dolls. Her eyes rolled each their own way but every now and then they levelled, and she thrust the pin in deep. The new doll, a big one with her eyes dyed dark with a root from the garden, and feet coloured scarlet for boots, had used up almost all of the pins she had left in her tin.

She kept refilling her pot tankard from her big copper jug. In the bottom of the jug sat black sloes, steeped in clear spirit. When she poured out the drink it was the colour of purple nightshade and it tasted strongly of autumn and brambles and dead leaves and it made her eyes water.

Then Vaskalia began to work on the other doll, the smaller one with the round stomach. She must give it a white baker's hat but, scrabble as she might, she found nothing white enough in her bits box to make one. Furious, Vaskalia spat in the fat doll's face and then hurled it at the hearth and stomped off to bed. The metal springs groaned as she launched herself on to her bulky mattress. Every night she took a long time to settle. Tonight seemed even longer to her son Simlin. He sighed as he heard her rolling over and over and muttering to herself, 'Keep it hidden. Keep it safe!' while the bed jangled and twanged beneath her.

Soon Simlin heard her piggy snores and whistles and knew it was safe to come out. He crept around, searching for scraps. Apple cores, plum stones, bits of gristle, shinbones, grease skimmed from the table top, anything would do to feed the hunger that twisted in his belly. His mother kept most of their food for herself, because she said Simlin must not feed the long white wiggly worms that fixed themselves inside his tubes. All he got to eat were scraps tossed from her table.

He scrambled up the wall to the rafter and hand over hand travelled along it like a speedy sloth. No titbits. His hand felt a furry skull with a narrow pointed nose. His fingers traced the cold eyes in the sunken face. It had been a fast dark fox, running across the hillside, its bushy tail behind it. There was a white fox skin, too, snowy and limp now. Vaskalia had skinned these creatures and set glass eyes in their hollow heads. She draped the limp bodies around her neck if ever she went out, to keep herself warm. When Simlin was little their empty skins and glass eyes in their sharp faces terrified him, but now he just felt sorry. Poor empty foxes, without their insides.

He hung by his feet and examined his mother's dolls on the high shelf. He picked up the baker doll and sniffed it. It should smell of sweet bread, but it smelled of his mother's sloe drink instead. Simlin had often sniffed with longing that sweet morning smell drifting down from the baker's tall house. He wondered what it tasted like, those things the baker and the ogress cooked. He put the baker doll back and dropped lightly down to the floor. As he was crouching by the fire he saw a small skeleton among the dry wood. He pounced upon it and gnawed it like a squirrel with a nut, but Bone Cracker had already picked away the last scrapings of flesh. Simlin threw it away from him in disgust and sprang onto the table. He leaned over and reached up on to the shelf again. His hand closed round the glass ball. He lifted it down and spat on the glass. He smeared his spittle all round the ball and rubbed it on his sleeve. The ball went cloudy and would not let him see what was inside.

Simlin's legs wobbled. He almost lost his balance and teetered on the table, clutching the ball tight. He mustn't drop it! He got himself right again with his slight weight on his two long feet. Then he climbed down carefully and squatted by the fire, so that its light shone on the glass.

Stupid mother! She had forgotten how she got the glass ball. She had not told that big woman the real story. Simlin knew the story and it was different. The glass ball did not belong to his mother's family at all.

When Simlin was a baby, Vaskalia kept him in a box. He grew bigger. He managed to open the lid. He started to crawl and then toddle. His mother kept ramming him back into the box and forcing down the lid. For a while Simlin gave up the struggle and decided that all little boys lived in boxes.

When Vaskalia went to the market place and set out her stall of spells and potions, she kept Simlin underneath, packed into a wooden crate along with onions and turnips from her garden. One morning he heard something come rumbling down the cobbled street and struggled up from the middle of the vegetables.

A ball came rolling down the hill. It dropped into the gutter and rolled on like a pinball in a game. It was shiny and lovely! Simlin squealed with excitement.

The ball stopped. The gutter was dammed by fallen leaves from the ancient walnut tree which stood in the very centre of the village, keeping the market place free from creepy-crawlies and flying insects. The ball could roll no further. The sun glinted on the glass. Vaskalia heard her son mewling and scrabbling in his box and bent down, ready to cuff him around his head, but he held out his hands to that ball glinting in the gutter.

Looking quickly from side to side and all around, Vaskalia scuttled across the cobblestones and grabbed the ball. She stuffed it up under her blouse like a third breast, and bound it to her body with scarves.

'Mine! Mine!' gurgled Simlin but his mother fetched him a sharp smack on the ear. She packed up her stall, scooping the vegetables, potions and pills and price lists of charms into the onion box on top of him and stomped home fast, the box held on her hip with the bawling, snotty Simlin inside.

Simlin never got to play with the glass ball. It lived high up on the shelf. His mother wedged her horrid dolls round so that it could not roll away, because it kept trying to leave. Every night she took it down and gazed into it, crooning. He heard her whine, 'My love, my love!' Who was she talking to? Not him, that's for sure. He had heard the word 'love' years ago at school when the teacher read stories to them. He had never heard his mother say 'love' when she talked to him.

She would not let Simlin hold the ball. He did, secretly, when Bone Cracker was night hunting and his mother was asleep.

Then Simlin had some freedom. He climbed around the five walls and examined everything on the shelf. Each night he gazed into the ball. Sometimes he saw monstrous things, slimy worms with no eyes. Once he saw a wolf with a skinny head and slavering jaws but he did not tell his mother.

Simlin was beginning to suspect that his mother could not see what he saw in the ball.

Now he rolled the ball gently across the floor. It came to a halt, rocking slightly. Simlin picked it up again and put his face right up close. His spittle had cleared. He could see a little boy trapped inside, asleep. Or dead. Behind him there was a shadow. It was so faint that Simlin could not see what it was at first, but as he stared the shadow grew a clear outline. It was a big creature with a broad, powerful chest and great shoulder bones like axe blades and a long, long tail. The creature was awesome. Simlin's mouth dropped open even further than ever.

Simlin rolled the ball again. That was the little boy from the orphanage. The boy with the big swaggering brother, the one who'd slapped him at school years ago.

Dare he do it? Simlin took a deep breath, picked up the ball and threw it down as hard as he could.

The seeing ball shattered. The pieces glittered like splinters of ice. At once Simlin was terrified. He dragged open the door and tottered outside. The daylight hurt his eyes.

He heard a scratching sound and blinked upwards. A shape crouched on the roof. The Bone Cracker had finished its night's hunting and now it was waiting to come in, shifting from foot to enormous scaly foot. Simlin crept into the garden. The snow was losing its crispness and his bare feet sank into mush as if he was in an icy swamp. He hid among some brambles and spied from safe inside the prickly cage.

The Bone Cracker flopped down off the roof. Simlin watched it shuffle in through the door. It would be going to roost on the rafter, to sleep off its heavy meal.

Simlin could just see in to the dark inside. Splinters of glass glittered on the earth floor. As Simlin watched, they began to move. They drew closer and clustered tight together again, fitting as exactly as a miraculous glass puzzle.

Then he watched the seeing ball roll out of the door, along the path and away down the road towards the sea.

CHAPTER 21

HONEYCOMB CAVE

It was the silence that woke Jez up.

Instead of the damp plaster walls of his home, there was a great expanse of sky. He struggled to his feet and saw that he was on a ledge. Below him, a dark stream wound through the rocks like an adder. Across it were seven pale islands. Now he remembered. They were stepping stones. He saw trees too, and the denser shapes of evergreen trees down in the forest. He was so high up he felt dizzy.

He could see everything clearly. It took him a moment to realise why.

For the first time in months, the snow had stopped

falling. Jez filled his lungs with clean, cold air and it made him cough.

He remembered that the owl had brought him here last night. He would never have found his way without it. Where was it?

It's daytime. Maybe it is asleep somewhere, like a proper owl should be.

Jez set off along the ledge, nervous about looking over the edge in case he lost his balance and fell off. He came to the mouth of a cave and stood there, shifting from foot to foot, trying to get the feeling back in them.

At last he made himself enter the cave.

The dark in the cave was thick so that Jez felt he could plunge his hand right into it and feel its softness. It lured him in. It scared him, too. The cave was like a great gullet, waiting to swallow him up. Yet it looked dry in there. He couldn't see any snow, or puddles, or dripping from the roof. Jez stepped inside. He looked up and gasped. The ceiling was vaulted and glowed as if it was sprinkled with stars. Stalactites hung like stone tears.

As Jez looked round, his eyes saw that there were small caves leading from the big one, galleried into the rock like a honeycomb nursery kept by monstrous bees. Each little cave sparkled.

On the cave floor were the embers of a fire. Jez caught the faint scent of wood, but that was overtaken by a much stronger scent of something alive, something he almost recognised.

He heard breathing. Fast, light breathing. His eyes were seeing more and more in the darkness and they kept going back to one round cave on the left.

Jez took a small step forward. He looked into the darkness. Nothing. Until, in an instant, two gold stones lit up, brilliant nuggets of hard gold set in black, shining hard at him.

Jez could not move. Out of the darkness formed the shape of a huge cat, reclining on the ledge. Its eyes held him. They drew him into a world of wildness, without people, with nothing he knew in it. *Run! Run!* The alarm clamoured in Jez's head, almost hurting him. *Run!*

But he couldn't. He was locked into those eyes, helplessly, as if he had been hypnotised.

The creature lowered its round head. It nuzzled something by its side. Then it turned its gaze back on Jez as if to say, *Look what I've got* . . . A small bundle formed itself in Jez's sight. Against the cat's side lay the shape of a child, curled and still.

'Luka!' cried Jez and the word echoed in and out of the honeycomb caves, *Luka! Luka!*

Luka's body lay against the big cat in the cave. His face was pale as ashes in the fireplace early in the morning. Jez blinked. It was Luka's shape, in Luka's clothes, but Jez knew at once that Luka was not in there. Jez thought, Luka is gone. His body is like a coat he has taken off and left behind.

Jez longed to pick up the boy shape and hold it close to him. He stole glances at the big cat, not daring to stare. It took his breath away. It was far bigger than any cat could ever be. Its paws were huge and round with a bunch of short toes, and the plump soles underneath the paws were furry. Yet Jez knew those furry paws concealed sheathed claws as deadly as scimitars. He knew that those soft lips might suddenly draw back to reveal teeth capable of ripping him to shreds.

The white leopard did not bother to get up. It was so sure of itself. It watched him with its gold nugget eyes, never blinking. Lithe muscles rippled under its skin and Jez heard its quick predator's breathing.

Jez felt the leopard's eyes draining him of his fear. He stepped forward, carefully, first one foot then the other, until he reached it. He bent his knees softly and slid his arms under the body of his brother. The leopard rumbled deep in its throat. It did not get up, but the tip of its tail twitched. It held Jez in its gaze as he straightened up, lifting Luka's body, light as a bundle of twigs. Jez stepped backwards as if he were in the presence of a mighty emperor. Still the crystalline eyes held his, locked tight.

Jez edged his way back out on to the ledge. The daylight dazzled him and he stood, with Luka in his arms, blinking. He heard a growl from inside the cave, followed by a soft sound as the leopard dropped down to the floor. He heard it padding after him! Out it came, on to the ledge. He saw its pale otherworld eyes change in the daylight, its pupils shrinking to black slits in the golden centre.

A dog barked. Shocked back into his familiar world, Jez glanced over the edge of the ledge. A dog was splashing across the stepping stones of the stream. Behind her hung a mist of lean grey shapes. Wolves.

And further down the hillside was a black matchstick figure, head down, looking for tracks. It prowled steadily through the snow. Even at this distance, Jez could see the rifle slung across its back.

The dog and the lean grey shapes splashed through the stream, then stopped and turned. It was a wolf pack, with an honorary wolf. *His dog!* The pack had one mind. They were watching the man with the rifle on his back. The leader wolf lifted his narrow head and howled. A second joined in, with a note slightly apart. One by one the seven wolves sang their parts in a drear chorus like a bundle of long, limp reeds.

They stopped their howling as suddenly as they had begun. Jez felt something unfamiliar touch his face. Warmth. His eyes became weak and watery so that he had to close them.

He turned to the east and opened his eyes. Everything went black. He blinked quickly. The eclipse on his eyes cleared and he saw, floating above the earth just under a veil of cloud, a silvery yellow lantern.

Suddenly it broke cover! It surfaced and shone. Jez squeezed his eyes tight shut, feeling tears running down his face. The sun! He thought it had deserted them forever.

The clouds raced away, leaving behind them a sky so vivid it made Jez gasp. He cradled his brother tight. If he held him so tightly, his own body warmth would flow into Luka and bring him back to life, surely. He pushed back the hat from Luka's forehead to let the healing sunshine touch it.

To the east the sky at the horizon was streaked with waves of pink and turquoise and lemon, as if glass had been painted with thin colours. Over to the west it was as intense a blue as the gentian flowers that grew among the mountain rocks.

Jez felt a monumental shift, as if the world was turning faster, trying to make up for lost time.

And then he heard a low growl. He had forgotten all about the leopard! He heard the quick *chuff chuff* of its breathing and smelled the strong cat-smell of its fur.

Slowly, as if he was sleepwalking and did not want to wake, Jez turned round and looked. The leopard crouched, gathering its strength, ready to spring. Jez saw how low its belly was to the ground. He saw a muscle twitch beneath its skin and the tip of its great tail flick.

A shout! Jez turned and saw the man down the hill struggling to take off his gun and raise it to his shoulder.

'No!' he screamed. 'No!'

And the leopard sprang. In perfect grace, it leaped, with its tail streaming out behind it like a sail to balance the leap. It landed soundlessly on the rock above the ledge. It looked back at Jez and the limp form in his arms, quite unaware how beautiful it was, and Jez understood now that they were free to go. He set off along the ledge, treading as carefully as he could because the melting snow made the ground treacherous. He paused by the river. The ice was thinning and splitting. It looked like broken glass. Rills of meltwater trickled through the frozen crust as the ice yielded to the thaw. On the stepping-stones the snow had melted. Now they gleamed silver blue.

Meltwater raced down the mountainside with Jez, making dark rivulets in the snow. He careered along the edge of the forest. The trees were darkening as at last their branches shed their melting burden. Snow flopped to the forest floor in great wet dollops. Jez stopped short, almost dropping his brother. Blood starred the snow. His eye followed a trail of dark crimson drops to a clump of bloodied feathers.

Jez thought of the owl with the carriage lamp eyes. He remembered that bad dream, and the disturbance in the trees, the sound of wide wings. A sob caught in his throat.

He set off again, lurching from side to side down the hillside.

'Jez! Wait!' A figure was battling through the snow towards them. It waved.

'Dimitri!' When the baker caught up with them, Jez felt the hand that had squeezed his heart with fear of losing Luka relax its grip at last, and he began to cry.

'Let me see him,' whispered Dimitri. He laid his hand on Luka's forehead, then on his neck. He said nothing, but turned and stared up at the hillside.

'Look at it!' shouted Jez. 'Look at it now!'

The leopard was bounding away up the hillside, the dappled fur shifting across its back like rings of water in the sunlight. Just behind the leopard ran seven lean shapes. A little way from them loped a hare, her long ears tipped with black and her strong fur tipped with thistledown. Jez put his hand up to shade his eyes from the unexpected bright light. Was that something fluttering to keep up with them? Or were his eyes still bewildered by the unfamiliar sun?

As the creatures ran easily together, Dimitri and Jez saw that the snowline had crept further up the mountain. They wondered just what they were watching. They had to shake their heads and look again. Slowly Dimitri took the rifle from his back and dropped it in the snow. He cried, 'Someone is up there, Jez!' and he put his hand up to his eyes to shade them from the sun. 'Look! Far in front of them . . . No, it must just be a trick of the light.'

Jez watched as the snow disappeared almost before his eyes. It was as if someone was wearing a cloak of white, and was striding away from them, with the cloak billowing out behind him, pulling away. Further and further the cloak of snow retreated.

In its place, where the snow cloak had smothered the

land, appeared the colours of the earth, soft colours of green and gold, purple and brown.

'We are forgiven,' said Dimitri, but Jez thought, The Earth is looking after itself. Despite the war, the land and the rivers and forest and the creatures will survive somehow. Even without us.

The leopard bounded out of sight and Jez felt Luka stir in his arms.

CHAPTER 22

THE INVISIBLE WALL

Simlin ran after the glass ball as it rolled down the road. His sides ached with his running. The ball would not wait for him! It did not want to be caught prisoner again and taken back to the house with five walls.

The road was wet. Meltwater was trickling down from the mountains, gurgling in the gutters and soaking the earth as the heavy snow dissolved in the sunshine.

'Garden!' gasped Simlin, puffing along the road, because his mother would sleep until noon and her garden would flood. She would rage, but what could he do? Serve her right. He loped on down the road, past the inn missing its top storey. He had heard that the road went towards something they called the sea. The sea must be that sheet of iron he could see from the top of the orphanage. If you went the other way, you came to the mountains. What were mountains like, close up to you? Would they spit at you? What was a sea? Could you eat it?

'Never know!' he wailed.

He could go no further. She had put an invisible wall across the road. Simlin hit the air with flat palms, then with his angry little fists. He couldn't go past this wall and could not break it down. His mother had built it with a spell. What would she do to him now?

'Break her!' he cried. 'Be free, Simlin!' He turned and drove his shoulder hard against the wall. The wall pushed back and sent him spinning along the road as if it had whipped a top. He battered it up and down, ran to and fro, searching for a way through, but the wall completely blocked his way. Simlin spun helplessly round and round, wailing. He slowed down, clutching his bruised shoulder. His mother's power was strong as stone. But there was the ball, wedged up against a fallen branch. Quick! He threw himself at it and peered close.

No, boy, now . . . take it back . . . go back . . . It was his mother's voice. She had always told him what to do, every minute of the day, nagging and screaming at him, even if she wasn't there. Simlin picked up the seeing ball and turned back, his heart heavy as lead under his skinny ribcage. His splayed bare feet were blue with cold. Filthy water swirled around his skinny ankles, slopping coldly on his skin and leaving a crust of dirt.

He talked aloud to himself as he slopped along.

'Simlin! Get power. Wear shoes so feet don't get wet. Run away down the big road? Can't. Mother made the wall to stop you. No escape. Get important, Simlin, get important. Matter to people. Matter to Mother! Find the thing she hides, the thing for the blind boy's gift, steal it for self, get power for you. Then Mother will love Simlin.'

CHAPTER 23

THE SHADOW OUTSIDE

'KATRIN! Get the door OPEN and the kettle ON!' The bolts slid, the door opened and Dimitri ushered Jez and his armful inside.

Jez put Luka gently on the long trestle table. Katrin ran upstairs for blankets and Dimitri hurried to build up the fires so that the flames leaped. Big Katrin bent over Luka, stroking his forehead, while she listened to Dimitri's hurried tale of seeing the boys and the great white leopard.

'No of course I didn't shoot it, Katrin!' he said, thinking, But I almost did!

Katrin put her fingers on Luka's neck, feeling for his

pulse. Her eyes were dark wells full of sadness. Dimitri could not bear to look into them. If he did, he might drown in that grief. The village must not lose another son. All they could do was wait.

Jez pulled up a chair close to the table and sank down on to it. He leaned over his little brother. He whispered, 'I don't know what happened, Luka. I don't know how you ever got into that cave. All I wanted to do was to bring you back. And I have!'

'I don't understand why that leopard creature didn't attack you, Jez,' said Dimitri. 'Why was it down from the mountain? Where was it hiding? How did you find them?'

Jez held up his hands to stop the questions. He felt light-headed. It was a good feeling, the relief of coming back to people he loved and things that he knew. Routine! He hadn't liked the strange journey, but at last he had taken off his heavy belt with the sad little metal images and laid it aside.

The bakery door opened and in hurried Imogen, smiling. She spoke softly to Dimitri, asking where they had found Luka.

'Jez found him!' cried Dimitri. 'In a cave, miles away. He rescued him from the wild beast. Jez is a hero, Imogen!'

'I know he is!' she said, and Jez felt his face blush.

'Has anyone ever told you your voice sounds like a cello, Imogen?' said Dimitri suddenly, and she laughed. Jez had never heard a cello and did not know how it sounded, but he knew that Imogen's voice sounded soft and beautiful.

Jez said carefully, 'I know it sounds strange. But I don't think Luka was in danger from that leopard. It was almost – watching over him. I wish he would wake up now. I don't know where his mind is . . .'

'Sssh, Jez, I'm sure he'll recover, now he's back with us,' whispered Imogen.

Katrin brought hot tea. The four of them cradled the cups in their hands and sat in silence, looking at each other, looking away, looking at Luka, and then watching the fine flames in the fireplace. It was a precious silence.

Big Katrin's mind had been turning like a mill wheel, churning out ideas and thoughts. She had decided that Jez and Luka should move into the rooms above the bakery. It was warm. They would be safe. Dimitri could look after those boys if she helped him, but he must think it was his own idea, or he might argue with her. Katrin went upstairs. She opened drawers and pulled out eiderdowns, blankets and pillows which had lain unused for years.

After a while Dimitri followed her to see why she wasn't preparing food.

He looked at the bedding spread everywhere.

Then he clapped his hands and laughed. He pounded down the stairs two at a time and danced across the bakery floor, shouting, 'Jez! Why don't you move in here?'

'Eh?'

'You're more than welcome. It'll be like having two sons. I get them ready-made! I won't have to spend all those years changing nappies and being woken up in the night first!'

Big Katrin staggered downstairs with bedding. She let down the wooden racks that hung from the ceiling and spread the sheets and blankets over them to catch the warm cinnamon air.

'If you are getting sons, then you had better get yourself a wife, Dimitri,' said Imogen slyly. She and Jez both looked pointedly at Big Katrin, who refused to respond and concentrated on smoothing out a pillowcase.

'Why doesn't Big Katrin move here too?' whispered Jez to Imogen. 'She lives all on her own, doesn't she? She'd be safer here with us, and . . .'

Imogen shook her head and put her finger to her lips.

'I could easily get myself a wife!' cackled Dimitri recklessly. 'I've got a girlfriend in a little shack up the road, but her eyes make me feel funny and my lips turn green when she kisses me!'

Then he wished he'd kept quiet. Supposing Vaskalia found out that he had mocked her? He quickly changed the subject. 'We'll get back to normal tomorrow. We'll bake lots of bread, even if it is made with powder yeast. Yes, Katrin, I found that pot of yeast you'd hidden in the tea caddy. I don't approve of dried yeast, but then, needs must when the devil drives.'

He rubbed his hands together gleefully at the

thought of tomorrow's baking. 'I'd better build up the fires ready. It's thawing outside, Katrin! The rivers will be full and the miller will be happy because his water wheel will turn again, and he can get on with grinding his flour. Maybe people will come back to the village now the thaw has come? We'll have lots of customers!'

He took his wheelbarrow and went outside to the wood store. He gazed up and saw that the sky was sprinkled with stars. There was a white curve of moon. It was a clear sky now, free from snow clouds. Maybe spring will start and my swallows will return to nest, up in the rafters. Maybe I shall see their smiling faces . . . Dimitri opened the door of his wood store. How good it smelled. Oak and walnut wood, cherry, apple and pear . . . no old furniture rubbish or packing cases, only the best for this bakery! He sniffed deeply and then wished he hadn't, because there was that other smell again . . . almost as if Syrup had been in there. Dimitri loaded up the wheelbarrow with logs and pushed it inside.

The second he had gone, a shadow slipped out of the wood store. Keeping close to the wall, it stole into the street and ran off into the night. It was a panther, escaped long ago from a zoo in the south which had been bombed. It had been roaming around the village all winter.

By the time Dimitri returned to lock up, the panther was gone far into the forest.

CHAPTER 24

DANCING DAYS AHEAD

Luka lay still. He was listening to the bakery. Only moments ago he had been somewhere else, listening to the great cat breathing, to the clinking of the ice thawing, drop by drop, sounding like splintered glass. He had heard the melting water dripping from the snow as the long winter yielded and surrendered at last. Now he heard the rasping of Syrup's tongue as she washed her kittens, and the crackling of twigs on the fire. He heard the mewing of Syrup's kittens and the dog whimpering in her sleep as she dreamed.

He smelled cinnamon, and a cake baking, and the lavender that Big Katrin put in bedclothes. He felt warm and safe among people he loved. He heard the murmur of their voices.

Dimitri said, 'Come back to us, Luka. Wake up. Please!' But Luka had not the strength to answer him, even to open his eyelids. He had travelled such distances, down towards the earth and its monsters, alongside sparkling water that splashed over stones of pearl, up hillsides towards skies full of bowling clouds. There was no going back. He had felt his way, pushing through green glossy leaves and twigs thick with scarlet berries, into velvet darkness under a blue sky spangled with stars. He had felt the dense softness of that dappled fur and the big heart beating.

There was another rustling sound. It was Jez rummaging in his backpack. Jez shouted, 'Wow! Luka ate all the sandwiches I made him. And all the apples! Good!'

'*I fed them to the Cloud Cat from my dream, Jez.*'

Dimitri and Jez looked at each other. Then they looked down at Luka. His face looked just the same, but he had spoken.

'She was so hungry! I remember how greedy Syrup

got when she was full up of kittens. The Cloud Cat has two cubs inside her body, nearly ready to be born. She came padding down from the mountains to look for shelter and food, down into danger from men. Those drums I heard were heartbeats! One big heart, her own heart, and the two little ones. Now the weather is milder she can go back to her lonely places. She's very shy. She believes people will harm her and kill her for her coat. I'll go with her again one day. She cared for me and gave me her power. We needed each other . . .'

'Wow, Luka!' breathed Jez. 'When you are better you must tell me more about her, and I'll tell you all about a big owl that tried to guide me.'

In his mind Luka saw the owl. He felt such sadness for her. Luka realised now that the owl had come seeking him, hooting to him, wanting him to fly with her, but he had chosen the leopard. So she had gone to guide Jez to him. Now she was dead.

Jez was still talking. 'The story's over, Luka, and it's a happy ending. We'll come to live here with Dimitri and everything will be safe and sound and back to normal again!'

But Luka knew it would not be safe or sound or back to normal ever again. Things would never be the same. He was full of an extraordinary calm. He had always known that he was different, an outsider, the odd one out, and now he had discovered why. There was a power inside him. He could shift his soul into other creatures!

Luka wriggled with the joy of this secret. There were other places and beings for him, and if he could change like that, so could the everyday world. Already things were moving. The village had been frozen for months but now the thaw had begun. Perhaps people who had left would return?

Luka felt Jez smiling down at him. He opened his eyes wide and Jez looked right into the gold eyes of the snow leopard! He looked into their terrifying world of wildness, and backed away from Luka, shaking his head.

I'm going to need help looking after him now. He's different. He looks powerful! But he's still my blind little brother. I'll have to watch him all the time.

'At last!' cried Dimitri as Big Katrin cut into the coffee cake she had baked. It was sweet and moist, with creamy icing, and a fairy ring of walnuts on the top.

Dimitri ate three slices, smacking his lips. Then Katrin tapped him on the arm and pointed up at the tall cupboard.

Dimitri nodded. He fetched the three-legged stool. He climbed on and reached up to the back of the top shelf, coughing at the dust. He stepped down again carefully, with his fiddle and bow. He put the fiddle on his shoulder and tuned it, wincing at the squeakiness. When it sounded sweet again, he played the music that had been locked away in his heart for so long. Plaintive music. Love songs. Laments for the people who had gone over to the other side, and the people who were lost to them forever. Music for the sea, the mountains and the forests.

Nobody spoke. Big Katrin listened, eyes closed. Jez stared into the fire, the music flooding his mind. Imogen thought of her family. The music said everything they wanted to say, without words. The dog lay on her back in front of the fire, legs splayed, showing a round pink tummy. Syrup pinned down one kitten, washing it fiercely with her sandpaper tongue while the others licked the last bits of cake icing from the plate.

Now that Luka was returned to them and the thaw had begun, Dimitri knew the time to dance would come again soon. Everyone was far too tired to dance tonight but he played a jig, light and quick, to lift their spirits.

Just Luka stood up. He stretched out his arms to them all and a wide smile spread across his face. Then he began to dance.

To be continued . . .